LONDON
CONFIDENTIAL
#4

FASHION

Tyndale House Publishers, Inc., Carol Stream, Illinois

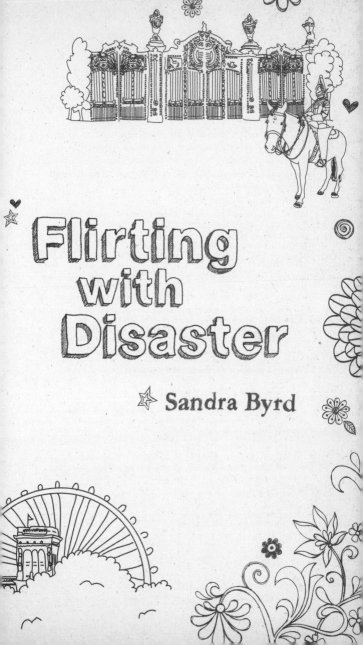

Flirting
with
Disaster

✦ Sandra Byrd

Visit Tyndale's exciting Web site at www.tyndale.com.

Visit Sandra Byrd's Web site at www.sandrabyrd.com.

TYNDALE and Tyndale's quill logo are registered trademarks of Tyndale House Publishers, Inc.

Flirting with Disaster

Designed by Jennifer Ghionzoli

Edited by Stephanie Voiland

Published in association with the literary agency of Browne & Miller Literary Associates, LLC, 410 Michigan Avenue, Suite 460, Chicago, IL 60605.

For manufacturing information regarding this product, please call 1-800-323-9400.

Library of Congress Cataloging-in-Publication Data

Byrd, Sandra.
    Flirting with disaster / Sandra Byrd.
        p. cm. — (London confidential ; #4)
    Summary: When forwarding a text message gets fifteen-year-old Savvy Smith in big trouble, she begins wondering if there is such a thing as luck and, if so, how it relates to God, but to find out she must put her advice column, her ministry, and her friendships at risk.
    ISBN 978-1-4143-2600-9 (sc)
    [1. Schools—Fiction. 2. Advice columns—Fiction. 3. Text messages (Telephone systems)—Fiction. 4. Luck—Fiction. 5. Christian life—Fiction. 6. Americans—England—London—Fiction. 7. London (England)—Fiction. 8. England—Fiction.]
    I. Title.
    PZ7.B9898Fli 2010
    [Fic]—dc22   2010026062

Printed in the United States of America

16 15 14 13 12 11 10

 7   6   5   4   3   2   1

FOR ELIZABETH BYRD,

my beautiful, smart, and funny daughter.
I'm glad we're thisclose. Happy sweet sixteen!

Chapter 1

Forward this to 10 friends within 2 hours & something good will happen in your life 2day and 2morrow. But if you don't then something bad will happen 2day and 2morrow. This is real and not a joke!

I rolled my eyes. *Hazelle, really?* She seemed so no-nonsense, I could hardly believe she'd fall for that kind of thing.

The text came in on Sunday night, just as I was getting ready to throw a load of clothes into the washing machine. I was surprised to get a forward from Hazelle—she hardly ever texted me.

I shut the washing machine lid and didn't give it another thought.

Mostly.

I went upstairs and strummed my guitar for a while, then texted with Penny, my bestie, and Gwennie and Jill and some of my other friends. In spite of myself, I kept glancing at the clock to see if the two hours had gone by. Then I reminded myself how stupid that was and went back to texting. After a while my in-box was full, so I erased everything in there.

With a start, I realized that I'd gotten rid of the forward from Hazelle. So now I *couldn't* send it on.

What does it matter? I asked myself. *I don't believe in that kind of stuff anyway.*

I brought down a second load of clothes, tossed the first one in the dryer, and threw a heaping scoop of snowy white laundry powder into the machine with the dirties. I shut the door, and the machine began to shake its hips and swirl my clothes back and forth like a hula skirt.

Later that night I headed downstairs to pull my wet clothes out of the washer. I untwisted them as I pulled them out.

"Oh no!" I shouted loudly enough that my mother could hear me over the telly she was watching in the next room with my father.

She came running into the laundry room. "What?"

I held up my jeans, my favorite jeans, the only jeans that fit me perfectly and helped me look effortlessly fashionable on no-uniform Fridays. Big white streaks ran through each leg like badly healed scars. I handed them to Mom and pulled out one of my favorite hoodies, one that my cousin in Seattle had given me just before we moved to London last year. Ruined. My bright pink Juicy jacket looked like it had permanent stains all over it.

"What happened?" Mom held up the jeans and clucked. "What did you put in here?"

I tapped the plastic tub of laundry detergent. "This."

"Ahhh, that's bleach powder, Savvy." Mom pointed to the larger tub in the laundry cubby. "This is the detergent. I'm sorry." She looked genuinely sorry, too—she knew the worst part of all was my jeans. They were the first expensive piece of clothing I'd bought with my own money. "At least your socks are really bright." She held up my white anklets.

"Big comfort," I said, wondering how I could have made such a mistake when I'd done the first load right. I gathered up the ruined wet clothes and tossed them into the dustbin.

As I went to bed that night, I lay there wondering how I was going to get the money to buy new jeans. I knew things were tight for my parents too—so tight that we weren't even going to leave London to visit Seattle this coming summer. My mom would buy me some Levi's, but I knew she wouldn't fork over the money for designer jeans.

I mourned the loss and thought how close the word *denim* was to the word *demon*. One last time I glanced at my phone, which was sitting on top of my closed Bible, to see if Tommy had texted (he hadn't) and then tried to push away fears about Hazelle's forward and future impending disasters.

Chapter 2

Even though we normally had our school newspaper staff meetings on Tuesdays, Jack had called one on Monday morning for some reason. Officially, I was only the paper delivery girl. Unofficially, secretly, I also wrote the popular advice column, Asking for Trouble. I was eager to get my own byline—soon, Jack had promised—but for now I was glad to be writing . . . and helping people. And as I was learning, deeds done in secret often had more power than the ones everyone saw. The plan had worked out well so far.

So far.

As Jack called the meeting to order, I stood as far as possible from Natalie, my evil nemesis. She gave me the dead fish eye, and I lobbed it back at her. Well, really. She could have Rhys, my former May Day Ball date who ended up going with her instead. They deserved each other. I didn't know why she disliked me, but the feeling was definitely mutual.

"Now that the end of the school year is approaching, we need to turn our minds to some serious business," Jack began. I still hadn't gotten used to the idea that summer break didn't start until July here. "As you know, next year I will be moving up to sixth form, and so will Melissa. That means the paper will need a new editor. By tradition, anyone who has been on the paper staff for a year or more is eligible for the position." Jack looked around the room, but his gaze lingered just a second longer on Hazelle and then on Rodney, the sportswriter.

"We'll be having elections sometime in June, date to be announced. As far as I can see, the election will be open to Hazelle, Rodney, and Alex, should they desire to have it. However, if you feel I've overlooked you and you'd like to be considered, please let me know right away."

He clapped shut his notebook. "With that, let's get back to business as usual so the next edition of the Wexburg Academy *Times* can go out on Thursday."

Everyone dispersed, and I noted that I had only about three minutes before the first bell. I'd been planning to talk to Jack about the article he'd promised I could write. I needed a deadline and a topic. I was so excited—the first article I'd be writing for the paper with my own byline. But Natalie cut me off and buzzed into his office, firmly closing the door in my face. I took a deep breath and bit back the words on my tongue. My question for Jack would have to wait.

I walked to maths with Hazelle.

"This has been an absolutely fabbo day already," she said. "My grandmother sent me a cheque for a hundred pounds, and my mum gave it to me at brekkers this morning. Brian sent me some great snaps of us at the ball. And now the editor election. I doubt if Rodney and Alex even want it."

I hoped today would be fabbo for me, too.

Chapter 3

At lunch that day I sat at the table full of Aristocats, the uber-popular group I hung on the fringes of, thanks to my friendship with Penny. Apparently they'd all received the same forward Hazelle had sent to me; I couldn't imagine who in the world they had in common with her. Although they only touched on the subject briefly before moving on to the next topic, Penny happily shared that she'd received an unexpected A on a science project and another girl had gotten her computer back from restriction early after they'd forwarded the text.

I excused myself early to try to catch Jack, who was sitting at the newspaper staff table, before he left. When I reached the table, I glanced at Hazelle and noticed she was poring over the horoscopes in a magazine.

"Hi, Jack. I'll, uh, have the column in to you tomorrow." I kept my voice low so no one would overhear anything about the Asking for Trouble column.

"Brilliant." He looked at me uncertainly and glanced up to wave at a friend. I could tell by the look on his face that he was wondering why I was telling him this. I had to speak up before he took off.

"I was just, uh, wondering about my article. The one you promised me when I took the photos at the May Day Ball. Do you have a deadline for me, a topic, word count, you know?"

He returned his gaze to me. "Oh yeah. I'd forgotten. Well, all that will be up to the new editor, right?" He flashed *that smile* of his at me, which didn't look at all appealing at that particular moment. "Gotta dash off, Savvy. We'll talk soon." With that, he headed off to meet the group of guys who seemed to be waiting for him.

Up to the new editor? But he'd promised!

As the students from first lunch left the room, everyone with second lunch began to stream in. I scanned the flow, trying not to look overinterested.

I spied Tommy as I was nearly out of the room. I didn't think he saw me, though. At least, if he did, he didn't wave or catch my eye.

Chapter 4

The second text came after I was already in bed. I saw the backlight on my phone, and I plucked it off the Bible, still closed, on my bedside table. It was a forward, this time from Monique, in my French class, with whom I had exchanged *mo-bile* numbers, as the Brits say.

This forward urged me to pass this message along to five people I cared about plus the person who had sent it to me. If I forwarded it, I would have four wishes come true. I sat there in the dark thinking for a while.

On the one hand, it *had* been really nice of Monique to send this to me. Like the text said, it meant she cared about me. I didn't exactly believe the superstition about something bad happening if I didn't send it on, but I didn't want her to think I didn't care about her too. We'd just started to become friends since Madame had changed our seats. Before I could overthink things, I quickly forwarded the message to the first five people in my address book . . . and to Monique. Then I closed my eyes and slept fitfully, with vivid and disturbing dreams.

Turned out I had no reason at all for that bad night's sleep.

When I got to school the next morning, I headed to the newspaper staff room first thing. Jack motioned me into his office and closed the door.

"I'm sorry I don't have the column to you yet," I started, thinking that's what he was going to talk to me about, even though it wasn't officially due till the end of the evening.

"I'm sure it'll be smashing, as always. Listen, Savvy—" Jack ran his hand through his hair—"I handled things a bit badly yesterday at lunch. What I meant is that of course you're going to be able to write an article, just as I'd promised. A real article, with a real byline. I'll notify the new editor candidates about it. We work together for a transition period at the end of the year, and I'll make sure we set aside some space for you in the paper, say, toward the end of June. I can have you work with Melissa on technique and research till then so you're ready. All right?"

"Thank you!" I beamed.

"Your choice of topic will have to be approved by the new editor. But that's nothing unusual for any journalist. Part of the job."

"Of course," I agreed, knowing that I could work with anything. *Would* work with anything. I was going to be a journalist. At this point, anyway, it seemed like Hazelle was a shoo-in for the editor slot. Alex, our typesetter, didn't seem like the kind of guy who would want to run. Rodney was a possibility, but my hunch was that he wouldn't get many of the girls' votes since he only wrote about sports. Hazelle and I had had a rocky start, but I felt like by now she would give me some freedom to write what I wanted. I floated through the rest of the day.

At lunch, Penny asked if I wanted to see a movie with her on Friday night.

In fifth period, Madame Antoinette assigned Monique and me to work on the same country project, which meant we'd be getting together to make a dish and find some music from Montreal for our part of the French fair at the end of the month.

"Thanks for sending back my text," Monique said.

"No problem."

"Have you had a good day, then?"

"Great!" And even then, I had no idea how great it was going to get.

After school, Tommy came up beside me as I walked down the hall with Penny. She knowingly dissolved into a group of other girls, leaving Tommy and me alone.

"How's your day been?" he asked.

I was very aware how close his head was to mine, his brown wavy hair nearly the opposite of mine, blonde and straight.

"Good," I said. "I'm going to be assigned a real article for the paper soon." Last month at church Tommy had discovered my secret, that I was the Asking for Trouble columnist. But he'd promised not to tell anyone, and I believed him. Other than Jack, he was the only person at Wexburg Academy who knew.

Tommy stopped walking and looked uncharacteristically nervous. "Well, our football team is playing a home game on Saturday," he started. "Have you been to a game yet?"

I shook my head. Football—what we Americans called soccer—was very popular here.

"Would you like to come this weekend?" he asked. "I know that Penny goes to watch Oliver. So it's not like you'd have to stay there alone while I was playing. And afterward, a group of us heads out to get something to eat together. If you're interested, well, I'd like for you to come."

Was he really asking me to go to his game and then out afterward? With others, of course. I wasn't allowed to date yet—single dates, anyway—but this was different. Surely my parents would see that.

"I'd love to," I said.

He leaned in thisclose and then touched my shoulder, brushing my hair off of it as he did. "I'm glad," he said. "Text you later."

Oh, my goodness. Best. Day. Ever.

Chapter 5

"Mom, Mom!" I yelled as I kicked off my shoes by the front door of our home, Kew Cottage, found at the heart of Cinnamon Street in the little village of Wexburg.

Predictably, Momlike, my mother came rushing to the door, probably alarmed at the intensity in my voice. As soon as she saw the grin on my face, her own face relaxed. "What's up, Savvy?"

My sister and her dog, Growl, came running around the corner. I flopped onto the couch, which the Brits call a lounge, and Growl, whose real name was Giggle, barked at me to let me know he was not amused by this false alarm, then retreated to his pillow.

"Tommy asked me to watch his game on

Saturday and to grab something to eat with a bunch of them after the game. Including Penny," I added to ensure that she'd say yes. Mom loved Penny.

Mom smiled. "Okay," she said.

"And I'm going to write an article for the paper with my own byline by the end of the school year."

"Great!" my sister, Louanne, said, her strawberry blonde French braid coming loose from the form I'd put it in before school.

"And Monique and I are partners for the French project."

"Bark!" Growl said. I reached over and patted his head. I was feeling mighty magnanimous. After a bit I got up off the couch, fixed a bowl of Weetabix for myself, and went upstairs to do my homework. All of this good stuff because I'd forwarded one little text!

Later that night I sorted through the questions that had been submitted for the Asking for Trouble column. I had to have it submitted to Jack by tonight so it would be ready for Thursday's edition of the paper. Normally I looked up a Bible verse that was the silent backbone of every answer I wrote for the paper. It was important to me that my answers be based on the Truth. Tonight I didn't even *need* to look up a Scripture that I would base my answer on. I knew this one by heart.

God works in mysterious ways.

Just like every other lesson God let me share with people, I'd had to learn this one for myself first. And if those text forwards weren't mysterious ways that God was working in my life, well, then I didn't know what they were.

I quickly tapped out my answer, e-mailed it to Jack, and went to bed. No restless sleep at all; I slept like a proverbial baby.

The next morning as I headed toward my first-period class, I noticed Natalie coming down the hall. It was clear we were not going to be able to avoid each other. I made a stone of my face and prepared myself to deflect her stiff hello.

"Hey, Savvy!" she said, warmth suffusing her face. "How are you?"

I practically fell over. I was, quite literally, struck dumb. Was this the same girl who had given me the chill two days ago in the newspaper staff meeting and who had stuck me with taking photos at the May Day Ball so she could go with my date?

"Fine," I answered warily.

"Okay. Well, have a great day," she said with a power-watt smile before breezing on down the hall.

As I walked into maths class, I saw that I wasn't the only one shocked at Natalie's transformation. Hazelle stared at Natalie and then looked at me. Then she grimaced.

Chapter 6

Every Thursday I showed up at school early to pack my designer bag with copies of the Wexburg Academy *Times* to deliver around campus. If it was an Asking for Trouble week, I'd stop to privately read my own column. I read everyone else's, of course, but my own first. I was pretty sure that's what we all did.

Alex helped me cram my green bag, the one Penny had scored for me at the Peter Chen photo shoot, and then I prepared to go distribute.

"Savvy, wait a moment," Jack called as he saw me heading for the door. "I have a brief announcement to make." Everyone turned to focus on him.

"This will be quick," he said. "I wanted to

make sure everyone knows we have a new candidate for editor. Hazelle is running, as many of you expected. And Rodney still has his name in the ring. But the other day Natalie approached me and reminded me that while she hasn't been here all of this year, she was on staff for the full year the year before. She'd like to put her name in the contest, and as she qualifies, I agreed. The vote will be held in approximately one month. I'll keep you updated as necessary."

With that, he turned back to his work. Hazelle's face had gone so white that her freckles bloomed. Natalie looked self-satisfied, like she'd just been grooming her paws and sharpening her nails at the same time. She grinned warmly at me, and I forced a smile back.

I went to deliver the papers, and afterward I sat down on a bench outside the office to read my secret column.

Dear Asking for Trouble,
One of my friends just started a business selling jewelry that she makes. She wants me to have a party and invite all my other friends over to look at the jewelry and maybe buy some. I guess it's a good

idea, but part of me feels nervous because my friends might feel pressure to purchase things they really don't want just because I invited them. But on the other hand, the jewelry is really cute. What should I do? The whole situation is starting to feel less like a party and more like a choker chain. Help!

Signed,
Rings Are Not My Thing

♡

Dear Ring,
I totally understand your situation. No one likes to use her friends, but everyone wants to share good things. Why don't you just send out the invitations? I mean, sending something out can't hurt, right? No pressure attached. Then if they want to come, they can show up; if they don't, you don't need to feel bad and neither does your jewelry-making friend. Who knows? Maybe your friends will find some really great accessories that they've been wanting and your other friend will

make some money. Everyone will end up happy! Things definitely happen in mysterious ways.

My pearl of wisdom . . .
Asking for Trouble

I closed the paper, satisfied that I'd offered good advice.

Just as I stood up, ready to make my way to first period, I sensed someone behind me. I turned to see who it was. Natalie.

"Hullo, Savvy."

"Hi," I said. Frankly, she this starting to feel a little stalkerish. At least Rhys was nowhere near.

"Reading this week's edition?"

I nodded.

"It's a good paper. But it's missing a little . . . spiritual dimension, don't you think? I mean, spirituality is such a big part of many people's lives. Including my own."

I'd once read that the face has like forty-three muscles. I was working really hard to keep all of them from displaying my complete disbelief. Wasn't this the person who, last month, had rudely brushed off anything that had a hint of religion? But I only said, "I agree completely."

"Good." The first bell rang, warning us that we had a brief three minutes to get to class. "I have just the person in mind to write a column like that . . . if I become the new editor, that is." She formed her forty-three facial muscles into a smile and headed to class.

Chapter 7

On Saturday I put on my best jeans—formerly my second-best jeans—and a baseball-style shirt that I thought looked sporty. I pulled my hair back into a long ponytail and restraightened it. After a quick retouch of my makeup, I was ready for my first date.

"This isn't supposed to be a date," Dad said as I came down the stairs.

I looked up, shocked. What, was he into mind reading now? "It's a group event," I told him. "Loads of people are going to be there." As I said it, I realized that *loads* was a British term. I was using those more and more now without even thinking about it. "And I'm paying for my own lunch."

Dad grunted and turned back to the telly, which featured a *Top Gear* rerun. Mom winked at me, and I went down the street toward the school.

When I got there, Penny was already sitting on the bleachers with some of the other Aristocats, including Ashley—who, I had to admit, still scared me a little. She was like a live electric wire. She could bring a lot of power, but she could also zap you bad if she felt like it. Her ladies-in-waiting were all cooing and billing around her, and she didn't notice me at all. Not that I was surprised.

"Hey, Sav." Penny patted the seat beside her. "Cute shirt."

"Thanks," I said, slightly paranoid that she hadn't mentioned the jeans. "I love your jeans," I told her. All right, it was weak—I was trying to prompt a response.

"Thanks." She didn't fall into the trap of returning the compliment. Drat.

All through the game she explained the rules to me, and actually, for a non-sporty person, I found it pretty interesting. I was surprised to discover that the players in British football loosely play offense or defense but don't have firm positions like in American football. Of course, my interest was mainly focused toward the home side of the field—where Tommy played—but I couldn't help it. For her part, Penny got a bit more animated when Oliver made a goal.

Afterward, it seemed the Aristocats were heading off to a party with Ashley and her boyfriend. Penny and Oliver were planning to go to a hamburger place in the village square with Tommy and me, as were a small handful of other footballers and their friends.

We girls moseyed over there first and scored a few long tables. I hadn't wanted to come to this resto before—it seemed clichéd to have the American girl hanging out at the hamburger joint and all that—but I loved it. The guys met up with us shortly after we arrived. Somehow, inexplicably, the seat next to me stayed open until Tommy arrived.

God works in mysterious ways! I rejoiced.

"Good game," I said as Tommy pulled out the chair beside me. It was obvious that he'd cleaned up—no mud clinging to him anymore. And I think he'd put on cologne. I was flattered. But it was also clear he hadn't done that too often. It was a bit strong.

"Hey, mate, heavy hand on the perfume,"

his friend on the other side of him said. Tommy blushed.

After we'd made conversation with the rest of the table, Tommy turned to me and asked about my guitar playing and what I was doing for my Tudor history project.

He looked interested in everything I had to say. It was very sweet.

The hamburgers were great, and after Tommy left with one of his friends, Penny's mom came and said she'd take us home. On the way out, I noticed Rodney, the sportswriter, sitting in a booth with a bunch of other people from school. A few of them were from the paper.

Natalie was with them.

I had no idea Natalie and Rodney were friends.

"So, good game," I said. "Busy weekend for a sportswriter, eh?"

"Right," Rodney said. "A win is always fun to write up."

"Having a little editorial competition too?" I teased, knowing that both Rodney and Natalie were running for the position.

Rodney shook his head. "I'm not running any longer."

I was surprised. "Oh . . . well, that's news."

He shrugged slightly.

"Bye, then," I said, and several at the table answered with good-byes of their own.

On the way out the door, I could almost have sworn I heard Natalie purr.

Chapter 8

After school on Monday, Penny invited me to come to her house to hang out.

"Normally I'd be right on it, but I've got plans today," I said. "Later this week?"

She nodded, and I headed home to quickly change my clothes and to pick up the writing notebook that Melissa, my mentor on the paper, had given me. I was preparing to research my first full-length article. I hoped that Hazelle—or Natalie, depending on who the new editor was—would let me write my piece about Be@titude, the local shop/ministry I supported. I wanted to be prepared just in case.

After a brisk walk to the square, I arrived at Be@titude. I looked at the window display before going in. The clothes were great—maybe a bit old for me, but really stylish. They'd be perfect if I had a job. And some Pradas. I pushed the door open, and the chimes jingled. The store was pretty quiet, as I'd expected for a Monday. That's why I'd chosen this day to come and ask Becky for an interview.

"Savvy!" Becky came over and hugged me like an old friend. "How are you? How was the ball?"

I grinned. "Long story." Becky had no idea that while I hadn't worn my beautiful tea green Faerie dress for the ball, I had worn it the next day, and everyone important had seen me in it. "I finally get to write a full-length article, and hopefully I can write it about your store and ministry. Do you have time for an interview?"

Becky checked her watch. "I do have just a few minutes, and then someone is coming in." A bright look came across her face, and she snapped her well-manicured fingertips. "Even better! One of the single mums we're planning to help with the new fund-raiser will be coming in to talk about her career aspirations and to be measured for clothes. That might make a good angle!"

Angle! Journalist speak. Melissa, my mentor at the paper, was going to be so proud when I showed up with a whole slew of good material to start with. "Sounds fantastic," I agreed. As Becky leaned against her glass counter, I flipped open my notebook to begin asking a few questions. "How did you get started in this business?"

"I've always loved fashion," she said. "But honestly, as a Christian, I sometimes felt like people viewed me as a bit shallow for caring about clothing and all that. I rather felt like it was putting my best foot forward and feeling good about myself. Later I thought how useful I could be helping other women feel good about themselves, especially at a time when they might be a bit low."

"Why single mothers?" I asked, hoping to not be overly personal but wanting to get to the heart of the ministry—and the article.

"My mum was a single mother," Becky answered matter-of-factly. "I know how hard it is."

As if on cue, the door chimed, and in walked a woman, her lovely face shadowed by fatigue. A little girl in a slightly too-small dress clung to one hand. The girl's other arm was curled snakelike around a little doll, ensuring that it wouldn't drop.

"Hullo," Becky said, warmly gathering them into the chic shop as if they'd always belonged. "I'm so glad you're here." She meant it—I could tell, and I saw they could too by the way their faces relaxed. "My friend Savvy is writing an article for her school paper on the shop and the ministry. Would you mind if she stayed for our interview?"

"You write for a paper?" the little girl squealed with delight. "And I'm going to be in it?"

"Hush, Emma." Her mother put her finger to her lips. But Emma looked up at me with such hero worship that I decided at that moment:

1. All little kids weren't the monsters I'd previously supposed. There were a few select exceptions to prove the rule. Emma was one of them.
2. I was going to get Emma into the newspaper. And laminate a copy of the article for her. And personally deliver it.
3. I needed to help this ministry. It was my calling, and I was going to make it happen.

Becky introduced me to the mother, Isobel, then took her to the back room to measure her. "I'll leave you in charge of the front of the shop, then," she said to me. "Just be helpful if someone comes in, and holler if you need me."

Me? In charge of the shop?

"Can you keep an eye on Emma?" Isobel asked.

"Sure," I answered nervously, remembering the babysitting disasters of Christmases past. And Easters past. And summer breaks past. I looked around nervously, but thankfully, no one came in. It wasn't long before I discovered a problem, though. Emma was missing.

"Emma!" I called out as cheerfully as I could.

No answer. I walked around the shop—it wasn't that big, after all—searching for her. Nothing. I turned the radio down to listen. Nothing.

Oh, Lord, I really don't want to go to the try-on rooms and tell them that I lost a child. But . . . I hadn't heard the door chimes. So she had to be in here somewhere. I went to a clothes rounder with blouses on it and parted a wedge to look inside. Nothing.

Dresses rounder, parted. Nothing.

Trousers rounder, parted. "You found me!" Emma said.

"Come on out," I pleaded.

"I can't," she said, seriousness creeping into her voice. "I'm playing house."

"Underneath the trousers?" I asked incredulously.

"I like to play house," she said. Then she crawled out, dragging her doll behind her. "But I'll come out if you want me to."

I closed the gap in the trousers, and the two of us sat by the register and played tic-tac-toe, also known as naughts and crosses, till Becky and Isobel returned, measurements in hand. After they left the store, Becky told me about some of Isobel's career goals and answered a few more questions for me.

"Next month I'm holding a huge Internet fundraiser," Becky said. "People bid on some donated items, and then at the end of the auction, I use the extra money to provide suitable work clothes for people like Isobel."

"Maybe I can help," I said.

Becky pursed her lips and sat quietly for a minute. "Sometimes the kind of help I'll need will be what you were just doing—child-minding, cleaning up, data input. Dull, I know, but critically important. But one other thing you could really help with is PR for people your age. Normally I get a lot of women in the shop, but unless there's a big event like the May Day Ball, teens tend to prefer Kensington or Oxford Street or Knightsbridge. Most teens have a pretty significant disposable income for clothes. If you could figure out a way to get them in here more than once or twice a year . . ."

"I'll think about it," I promised, but really, except for writing the one article—which frankly I'd be lucky to get permission to do—I had no idea what I could do to help. I gave Becky my number and gathered my bag and notebook before walking home.

Later that night, Becky called me. "Savvy, it's Becky. Listen, I'm sorry that I brushed right past your offer to help with the auction. Maybe you could come in once or twice a week till then and help with inputting things into the computer?"

"I'd love to," I said. That was something I could do. I hoped Becky would be very, very happy that she'd asked me to help.

Chapter 9

Wednesday night I headed to the coffeehouse at church. I'd been pretty busy the week before and hadn't been able to make it. Sometimes Tommy came, sometimes not, especially during football season.

My friend Supriya met me at the door. "Hey, Savvy! Mocha—whipped cream?"

"Definitely!"

We headed to the coffee cart, chatting and catching up while we waited. "New nose stud?" I asked. The stud in her creamy brown skin seemed a bit more pink than the last one I'd seen.

"Mmm-hmm," she agreed. "Gift from my grandmum in Mumbai."

We sat on one of the couches with a few other

friends to talk, when Joe, the youth pastor, came over and nudged me. "Hullo, Savvy. Listen, good news. We're going to need a guitarist on worship team in a couple of weeks. Are you up for it?"

I could see that Supriya looked delighted. Only a couple of months ago it had been my dream to play on the worship team at church, to be a part of leading others in worship. But now that the opportunity was staring me in the face, it sounded a lot scarier. Besides, I had another ministry that very well could take up a lot of my time, in addition to my main one—writing the column. "I'm not sure," I said.

Joe nodded. "Right. You'll want to pray about it. I totally understand. Well, let me know after you decide, okay?"

After Joe walked away, Supriya said, "Good idea to pray about it first. I'm sure that took a lot of self-discipline, 'cause I know how much you wanted it."

I smiled and didn't correct her. Prayer. Yes, that would be a good idea. I just hadn't thought of it. I really didn't think I needed to pray about this one, though. I was pretty sure I was on the right track.

After worship that night, someone came by

handing out flyers. I took one and glanced at it before sticking it in my Bible.

♡

As I was picking up my room before bed, a text came in. A forward. I didn't recognize the number, so I texted back.

Who is this?

Chloe.

Chloe? As in, the Aristocat who'd had a meltdown at the tea shop last month, which my mother and I witnessed? who had thrown her purse at the May Day Ball, scattering its contents, including Tommy's phone? who hated me because . . . well, because Tommy might like me?

Who had given her my number?

I quickly added her to my address book, just so she'd be in there for good and I'd know who she was if she tried to contact me again. She sent the forward again. I wrote back just to be uber-polite.

Hey.

But no way was I sending that forward on. Even if it did warn of bad news if I ignored it.

I was grateful I didn't believe in jinxing.

Chapter 10

Thursday morning I got to school early to deliver the papers. As I loaded the bag, I noticed Hazelle hunched over the new edition. She never read the paper on the morning it came out unless she had an article in it, and this week, she did not.

Okay, so I should have remembered that curiosity killed the cat. But I wasn't a cat.

"Whatcha reading?" I asked politely, jiggling the Peter Chen bag in order to fit in as many papers as possible.

"Nothing," she snapped.

Wow. I backed off.

"Oh, well, if you must know," she said, "my horoscope." She looked up at me. "What are you?"

I must have looked as dumbfounded as I felt.

I had no idea what she was asking. "A girl?" I offered.

"No, I mean, what sign are you?"

I shrugged. "I have no idea."

"When is your birthday?" she persisted. For some reason the whole line of questioning was starting to make me nervous.

"July." I didn't give her the date.

"You're probably a Cancer," she said.

As she spoke, Natalie quietly came up behind us. "That's not a nice thing to call your friend," she teased. "I think Savvy is rather nice, not a disease."

Hazelle rolled her eyes. "I mean her astrological sign is Cancer." She closed the paper. "I'm a Cancer too. Things don't look so good for Cancers this week." At that, she grabbed her book bag and made her way back to her desk, very clearly closing down the conversation.

Natalie smiled chummily at me and raised her eyebrows as if to say, *Well, what can we do?*

Against my better judgment, I found myself warming to her.

♡

First period I walked in just in time to witness a hostile look from Brian to Hazelle and the evil icicle she hurtled right back at him. At which point Brian turned to me and asked very sweetly, "Hey, Savvy, do you have a piece of gum?"

Now Brian and I had been gum-chewing buddies for months, but I wasn't about to get sucked into a lovers' Bermuda Triangle. "Fresh out today," I said, grateful that Louanne had pinched my last few pieces the night before.

The day didn't seem to be going well for Hazelle, Cancer or not. But for me? Fine.

On the way from third period to lunch, Chloe passed me in the hall. She flicked her gaze at me, but it certainly wasn't friendly. I was so glad I hadn't forwarded her text.

I sat at the newspaper table that day, chatting with Melissa about the article I was proposing. Natalie was sitting close to Rodney . . . but not as close as she'd been sitting with him at the hamburger place on Saturday. Hazelle was staring into her tuna fish sandwich. I wavered between feeling really bad for her and wishing she'd wrap the sandwich up before the smell permeated all our clothing. Feeling bad won, and I said nothing.

"Savvy?" Jack grabbed my elbow. "Can I have a word with you? In the courtyard?"

"Sure." I tossed my apple into the dustbin. It

landed with a heavy thud, kind of like my heart. When Jack wanted to talk in private, something was most likely wrong. I followed him into the bright May sunlight. We sat down together on a bench.

"Well, I don't know why it hasn't crossed my mind before now," he started, "but you do realize that we're going to have to let the new editor in on our secret."

I looked at him blankly. "Secret?"

"The Asking for Trouble column," he said.

Oh yeah. That. "Will I . . . Will I get to keep the column?"

"I dunno. The column is a great asset, and right now it's our most popular feature, given the amount of mail we get on it. But every editor gets to choose his—I mean *her* own lineup." He stood up to leave. "Just something to think about, okay? No need to say anything till after the vote."

I nodded and stayed on the bench, waiting for the bell to ring. In spite of her friendliness for the past two weeks, I still believed Natalie resented me because of my history with Rhys. Plus, she liked to be number one at everything.

She might want to write the most popular column herself—and take the credit.

Hazelle, on the other hand, would never forgive me for getting the column instead of her in the first place. Once she found out that her own sister, Julia, whom she idolized, had chosen me, she would never let me keep the column.

Suddenly, just like that, a thick cloud smothered the sun. I pulled my sweater around me and went to fourth period. I dug out my phone, scrolled through till I found Chloe's forward, and sent it on.

Chapter 11

Friday was no-uniform day. I loved it, lived for it—the day we could wear our own styles. Because the weather was warming up some, I wore my best pair of nonbleached jeans with layered tanks and tees over it and some Converse shoes. In Seattle I probably would have worn flip-flops, but even the relaxed dress code didn't allow for those here.

On the way to last period, Tommy came up alongside me. "Can I walk you to class?" he asked.

"Sure." We talked comfortably about our classes and last week's game. "I enjoyed watching it," I said. "My dad has become a real British football fan since we moved here."

"We play again tomorrow, but it's an away game," he said.

I felt a pang of disappointment that I couldn't watch it. "I hope you win." I stopped at my classroom. "One more class till Fishcoteque," I said, then immediately regretted it. Girl rule #109: don't bring up food with guys.

"I haven't been there in a long time," he said. "Mind if I join you?"

I grinned. *Cross off rule #109, ladies. Dudes like food.*

An hour later we pushed open the door to the steamy fish-and-chips shop, or chippie, as the Brits called it. Even though I was from Seattle—a seafood-lovin' town—I'd never liked fish till I moved to London. Here the fish consisted of firm little bites of moist flesh enrobed in a crispy crust and accessorized with tartar sauce or vinegar.

"What'll it be, luv?" Jeannie asked me. "The usual, then?"

I nodded, wishing she hadn't made it sound like I was here every day.

Tommy placed his order and then insisted on paying for mine.

"No, really," I said. What would my dad think?

"You can pick it up next time," he said.

That meant there would *be* a next time.

Tommy grabbed some napkins, and Jeannie leaned in close to me. "Dishy, that one," she said knowingly.

I didn't disagree. I smiled.

We sat and talked, mostly about church and how we both ended up there. "Joe asked me to play in the worship band," I shared.

"What did you say?" he asked.

"Nothing yet. I, uh . . . I guess I should pray about it," I said. "I'm getting really involved with another ministry."

"Sounds good," he said. We chatted and ate, and after a bit he said good-bye. I wished him good luck in his game the next day.

I finished my chips and orange Fanta and then grabbed the newspaper sitting on the next table. I turned to Auntie Agatha, my favorite column. After I finished reading it, I saw that the horoscope column was nearby. Funny, I'd never even noticed it was on that page before.

Before I could help it, I glanced at Cancer. "If you encourage someone you love, things will work out well for you," it said.

I pushed the paper away. And then a text came in. It was from Penny.

Savvy, Savvy, Savvy, call me right away. ASAP. With your mum nearby.

Chapter 12

I packed up my stuff and hoofed it the few blocks to Cinnamon Street and then raced inside. "Mom?"

"In here, Savvy," she called from the kitchen. Louanne was parked in front of the telly brushing Growl. One glance at his grumpy face and soggy paws told me that he'd been involved in some recent combat with Dr. Ruff's organic dog wash. By the looks of things, Growl had lost.

I called out a greeting to Louanne, who ignored me in favor of whatever show she was engrossed in, and I went into the kitchen. "Stay here," I instructed my mom. I saw the look on her face and added, "Please."

I called Penny. "Hey, Penny, it's me."

"Savvy! Has your mom checked her e-mail? My mum just told me she sent her a message a couple of days ago about the Chelsea Flower Show. It's tomorrow, and she wondered if she wanted to come. It'd be a good way to get to know the ladies in the garden club."

"Just a minute; I'll ask her," I said, ready to set the phone down.

"Savvy, wait!" Penny said. I pressed the phone back to my ear. "We get to come too. We stay in a hotel overnight, and we girls go shopping whilst the mums are at the show. I want you to come too!"

"Wow!" I said. "I'll call you right back."

I clicked off the phone and looked at my mom. This could be a really good thing . . . for both of us.

Chapter 13

Early the next morning Penny and her mum came to pick us up in their extremely cool little sports car.

"Nice to have rich friends," Dad muttered under his breath after he'd downed his morning breakfast of tomato juice with a shot of hot sauce in it. I grinned and kissed his cheek good-bye. He loved Penny. He was just jealous that he wasn't actually *in* the car or, better yet, *driving* the car. Instead he'd have to settle for watching *Top Gear* on the telly and taking Growl for a walk. He was a good sport about it all, though. I knew the hotel in Chelsea was more than we could really afford right now, and sacrifices would have to be made.

An hour later we drove up in front of the hotel,

got early check-in through our garden-show package, and met the others in the lobby. I noticed that Ashley's mother was in charge. No surprise. To my great relief, even though most of the others were Aristocats, Chloe wasn't there. At first Ashley thought maybe the ten of us girls should look at the gardens with the mums after all, but it was only because Ringo Starr had been at the show the year before, as had clothing designer Stella McCartney, and she was hoping to bump into some celebs.

She finally decided in favor of shopping on High Ken, as the locals called High Street Kensington, and then Oxford Street; the rest of us breathed a sigh of relief and headed down to the Underground. The concrete walls rumbled around me like they had in Seattle during an earthquake, and I reminded myself twelve times, under my breath, that my mother had said I'd never been claustrophobic. The Tube doors swooshed open, swooshed closed, carried us a short distance, and then we got off and raced into the late May sunlight. Shopping!

We bought some little things at Topshop—and I felt like an old hand there after having been, umm, once, officially—and then we were off to Bershka.

"Bershka?" I asked innocently.

Penny nudged me. Girl rule #212: Don't display ignorance of local fashion hangouts.

"Yes, Bershka. You know," Ashley insisted. "The Spanish fashion shop?"

"Oh, right. Bershka."

Ashley dropped £100 at Bershka, which was about $150 by U.S. reckoning, on a pair of tights and twice as much on a pair of shoes. We started down the street, and she announced, "I need some jeans."

I glanced at the store's slogan near the door: *Look Good, Pay Less.*

Hooray! I opened my little British flag snap purse and counted my money. "I could use some jeans too," I said. Maybe I'd find some to replace the ones I'd lost in the great washing disaster.

"Me too," another girl said. We looked at each other and smiled. When Ashley was involved, there was strength in numbers.

Ashley sailed through the various departments looking over all the jeans. At first we kind of trailed behind her like preschoolers crossing the street behind their teacher, and then we broke up and looked on our own. On one table I found the perfect pair of jeans. My size. Great stitching.

Skinny but not too skinny. Marked down. Just as I was about to pick them up and take them to the try-on room, Ashley announced, "There's nothing here I like. Let's go."

I noticed that the other jeans shopper had a pair in her hands too, but she dropped them like stolen merchandise within seconds of Ashley's announcement. I looked at Penny, ready to speak up and ask if anyone would mind if we waited a second while I tried these on. Penny shook her head a little to indicate that wasn't a good idea. I dropped my pair too, but I was steamed.

♥

Later that night Penny and I sat in our hotel room eating a room-service meal of roast and Yorkshire pudding in our pj's, and I asked her, "What was up with not trying on the jeans?"

"Ashley has some good points, like, uh, leadership, and she can be generous when she wants to. But she likes to be the boss."

Ashley, meet Natalie. That would be a smackdown I'd love to watch.

"So why do you go along with it?"

"I've known her since I was little," Penny said. "It's not worth it to make a big deal."

I was about to open my mouth and insert my foot—speak up about how she should stand up for herself—but as I thought about it, she *was* moving forward, a little at a time. Maybe I needed to step back a little. Then we'd be in step with one another.

Back home on Sunday night, Mom was helping me do my laundry—duh, couldn't afford to lose any more clothes—and we talked about the weekend.

"Hold on," she said, leaving the laundry for a moment to dash into the kitchen and retrieve a small, brown, leather-bound notebook with gold writing on the front. "Everyone got one of these to take notes in, even me. I jotted down quite a few ideas and made some sketches of what I could do in the back garden." She flipped through the pages, and I looked at them with interest.

Not that I was interested in flowers, mind you. I was interested in being interested in my mom.

"And look," she said, "some photos I took with

my phone." She scrolled through a few, and I oohed and aahed at the appropriate moments. "Not as good of a photographer as you, I'm afraid, but it should be enough to help me see what I might want to do." She smiled as she closed the phone.

"So did they say anything to you about joining the garden club?" I asked.

She nodded. "Lydia, Penny's mum, said that, barring unforeseen circumstances, she sees no reason why I wouldn't be voted into the club end of next month."

"Great!" I said.

"Maybe."

I looked at my mom. "Why only maybe?"

"Well, with the book club, I wasn't sure they'd want me, but if they did, I knew I'd fit right in. This time . . . Well, we're not rich, Savvy. We don't have a huge estate. I'm just not sure."

Chapter 14

Monday after school I was supposed to be in two places at once: watching Louanne and helping Becky with some prep work for the online auction, which was only eleven days away. I decided to float an idea.

"Do you want to come to Be@titude with me?" I asked Louanne.

"A fashion shop?" She wrinkled her nose.

"We walk by the ice cream shop," I said. "I could buy you a cone on the way home."

"Sundae," Louanne negotiated with a firm smile. She knew she had me.

"All right, sundae," I agreed. "Get your stuff and meet me on the porch."

Two minutes later she appeared . . . with Growl on a lead.

"Oh no," I said, "we're not bringing him."

"Of course we are," Louanne said. "Part of watching me is walking Giggle. Right?" At that, the dog turned up his nose and pranced right in front of me before shaking his leash. *Great. An uppity dog and a sister who's turned to extortion.*

We walked through the village, the birds singing sweetly and the leaves unfurling on the trees. Louanne skipped on the cobblestone paths, and I had to admit, if I weren't nearly sixteen, I might have wanted to skip myself. Growl was behaving. All was right with the world.

When we arrived, Becky was bustling about with Isobel and another woman, so I stood outside the door with Louanne and Growl. Emma came outside to join us. "A dog! A dog! I always wanted a dog, but our flat is too small, Mum says." She ran over and gave Growl a tight squeeze around the neck. His eyes seemed like they were about to pop out, and he had a look on his face that said, *Get me out of here,* but he stood still while Emma petted and hugged him.

Louanne leaned over and whispered, "You were right about this little girl. She's nice."

I winked at my sister. Anyone who loved dogs would be all right with her. Plus, Emma was younger than Louanne, which made Louanne feel mature. And important.

A few minutes later, Becky ushered the women out of the shop and me and Louanne in. "But the dog . . . ," I began.

"Pshaw, it's okay. You'll be in the back room doing some writing for me. The dog will be out of the way."

Louanne grinned, but I barely noticed.

"In the back . . . writing?" I asked excitedly, hoping I'd heard her right.

Becky smiled. "Writing. Would you like to do some rough copy for the second-to-last e-mails I'll be sending out before the auction? Only, what, a week and a half till the big event? I figure I'll send one this week and then one just before."

"Thank you," I said.

She sat me down and pointed out a stack of designer catalogs. "I've tabbed a few of the items I'm going to be auctioning—one-of-a-kind pieces, which is what we're known for. Go ahead and write copy for each of those to put in the e-mail."

Writing copy for fashion? I thought I'd gone to heaven. I flipped through the catalog and stopped myself from drooling all over the boat trousers, khaki capris, and personal-fit jeans. Not to mention the custom-tailored LeSportsac bags. I stuck to clothes for women—women with money to bid up an auction to support Isobel. And Emma.

An hour later, Becky came up behind me, read the copy, and exclaimed, "Savvy, you've done a marvelous job. I think that'll be it for today. I'll massage the wording just a bit and send them out. Thank you so much. Back next week?"

"For sure," I said. And the next week, and maybe during the summer . . . if things worked out right.

Later that night, after buying Louanne a heaping 99, a British ice cream specialty of vanilla ice cream with a large Cadbury Flake candy bar driven into the middle of it, I got home, popped open a tube of Smarties, and began to write my Asking for Trouble column. I had a lot of homework this week, now that we were nearing the end of the school year. I had better get my column done early. I knew just the verse I was going to use.

God helps those who help themselves.

Chapter 15

Thursday morning I was a bit late, so I didn't have time to read my column before getting to first period. When I arrived, I was in for a surprise. Hazelle was in the seat next to me, and Brian was across the room.

"Um, what happened?" I asked, sliding into the desk beside her.

"Nothing," she said. But she looked really, really sad.

"Gum?" I offered.

"I don't *chew* gum, Savvy," she barked.

Okay then. Just for old time's sake, I'd ice down that burn and try one last time. "How's the book coming along?"

"I stopped working on it," she said quietly, and

then she opened her notebook and fiddled with the lead in her mechanical pencil.

Oh yeah. She'd been writing a romance. I'd messed up that one.

After school I walked around the campus to pick up the extra papers. I snagged one and read my article before going to the newspaper office.

Dear Asking for Trouble,
I have an art project due in a couple of weeks. It's a really important project to me because I want to send my drawing portfolio to art school next year. A friend of mine, who also likes art, asked if we could do the next project together. I know it would help her to work with me, but I'm not sure I would benefit by working with her. But then I'd feel selfish. I could do this one with her and the next one on my own. What should I do?

Sincerely,
Needs to Draw a Conclusion Soon

Dear Draw,

It's nice that you want to help your friend, but you're trying to let your own work shine in this project, especially since you want to be admitted to art school. And you're right—if she's so excited about art, she might need to get this done on her own. Maybe she'd really benefit from having to stand on her own for this project, just like you're willing to do. I say go it alone.

Sincerely,
Sounds Sketchy

Melissa had promised me she'd stay after school and help me learn how to do an upside-down pyramid news article structure and teach me how to seamlessly work in British style quotes. "So here's where you put the comma, then," she said as we hunched over her desk. She tapped a few times on the keyboard and, *voilà!* as Madame Antoinette would say. Things were looking good.

I cut and pasted a paragraph about Be@titude's origins. The *pièce de résistance* would be the sidebar showing how much money the auction made to buy business wardrobe items for mums in need.

Hazelle had left early, for once. Her *Vote Hazelle* sign over her desk had lost one of its thumbtacks and now swung like a loose limb on the corkboard. Natalie was still there, though. She came up behind us. Melissa turned her head away, sending a shot of grapefruit scent from her hair into the air around us. She didn't meet Natalie's eye.

"Working on Be@titude again, I see." Natalie's voice was chipper. "Didn't you want to feature it earlier this month?"

"As a part of the May Day Ball article we *were* going to work on together," I reminded her, but she didn't take the bait.

"Looks like a worthwhile piece," she said. "Can't wait to see it in print."

Was it just me, or did that sound like a promise?

Then she gathered up her books and closed her laptop before strolling into the hall. I could see Rhys waiting for her.

He glowered at me before putting his arm around Natalie and walking away.

Chapter 16

❀

My mom and I had made a deal. She'd do my laundry on Sunday afternoon if I'd clean the kitchen. That way I could keep my remaining clothes intact and still get my allowance. This weekend I was feeling so good about life in general that I decided to not only clean the kitchen but also shine up the bathrooms, run the vacuum, and help Louanne with the dog.

"Wow, I'm not sure what brought on this burst of energy, but whatever it is, I hope it's a permanent condition." Dad lifted his feet off the floor while I ran the sweeper through the living room and turned up *Top Gear* so he could hear it over the noise.

"New episode tonight?" I asked after finishing the house.

Dad looked surprised. "Yes, actually." I didn't tell him that Tommy loved *Top Gear* too and that he'd told me Sunday nights debuted the new episodes.

I even drew a truce with Growl. I fed him treats while Louanne groomed him. Then, after taking my cleaned and folded clothes upstairs, I sat in front of the computer at the little office nook in the kitchen to do some homework. I quickly ran through my e-mail, not wanting anyone in the room to see that I'd been getting the forwards for the Asking for Trouble column. I'd read them later on my laptop. However, one message caught my eye. It was from Hazelle.

The subject line was "Tips for writers," and it had also gone to Melissa, Jack, and a couple of others on the newspaper staff. Not Rodney, though, and not Natalie. No surprise there. Hazelle was finally including me in a group of writers!

"Who's that from?" Mom asked.

"Hazelle," I answered. "It's an e-mail for writers."

"That's nice."

"I guess so. But she's never really included me in writerly things."

"Well, maybe things have changed," Mom said.

Yeah, like she knows the vote for editor is coming up soon. I clicked on the next e-mail. It was from *Ashley.* I gasped.

Mom came up behind me as she heard the gasp. "What's the matter?"

"There's a message from Ashley. She must have gotten my e-mail off a forward from Penny or something."

"What is it?"

"A forward. If you send it on to ten people plus the person who sent it to you by the end of the day, you will know your true love within a week."

Dad piped up from the next room, "You don't have a true love. You're not even allowed to date!"

"Turn the volume on the telly up, Dad," I called back.

Mom remained still behind my chair for a minute before speaking up. "Hmm. I don't know if I'd advise that. Maybe your friends don't want all these forwards. People get kind of annoyed with forwards, Savvy."

I rolled my eyes. "Not in my generation. We're

used to it. It's only the technological dinosaurs that mind them. We know what we're doing. Plus, Ashley will totally know if I don't return it to her. And she'll be mad."

Mom looked down at me and shrugged. I could tell she hadn't changed her mind. I hadn't changed my mind either.

"Has her mom or Penny's mom talked to you about the garden club yet?"

"Not exactly. But I did get an e-mail from Penny's mom, and it was sent to the whole garden club. I'm not sure what to make of it. I'll forward it to you and you can let me know what you think."

"Okay." I turned back to Ashley's forward and stared at it. I really didn't know what to do.

Chapter 17

"Are you going to Be@titude?" Penny asked me at lunch on Monday. "Or do you want to hang out after school?"

"I'd love to. I'm not going to Be@titude until Thursday—the day before the fund-raiser. I'm going to help Becky finish up the e-mails and send them out for her. So I'm open today!"

After school we walked down the streets of Wexburg to Penny's house. Well, *estate* would actually be a better word, even though it was called Hill House. Her housekeeper—yes, house-keeper—opened the door and let us in. "Hullo, Miss Penny," she said, her graying blonde hair pulled back in a serviceable bun. "And who's your friend?"

"This is Savvy," Penny said. "Mrs. Simmons," she introduced her back to me.

"Pleased to meet you," I said.

We went upstairs and sat on Penny's floor. A few minutes later Mrs. Simmons brought up some milk and warm cookies—biscuits, as the Brits say. This was the life. I started daydreaming. I'd be writing for the *Times* of London. My weekly column would be a huge hit. So huge, in fact, that one day an agent would call me at the office and offer me a book contract that would pay enough for me to buy a Hill House of my own. Complete with a Mrs. Simmons, who would always have hot cookies for me and my friends. . . .

"Savvy!" Penny jiggled my arm. "Are you okay? I've been talking to you for like a minute and you haven't answered. Plus, you just got a text."

"Sorry!" I said, reemerging into the real world. I looked at my phone. "It's from Hazelle." I scanned it. "Just a little note reminding me that there's a newspaper meeting in the morning."

"Oh," Penny said. "Is she the new editor, then?"

"Not unless Natalie gave up, and that's about as likely as sharks swimming up the Thames. The election is in two weeks. Just before the last few weeks of school."

"So you're going to vote for Hazelle, then?"

I nibbled the crispy, buttery edge of another cookie and let the warm chocolate melt across my tongue. "I don't know. Natalie says she'd let me write a column about spirituality."

Penny's eyebrows shot up. "She said that?"

"Almost." I plucked a third cookie, promising myself I'd forgo my weekly pilgrimage to Fish-coteque on Friday. "And she said she liked my Be@titude article idea."

Penny's eyebrows remained raised. "And what about Hazelle?"

I shook my head. "Brian dumped her, I think. She's really low about it. Didn't see that coming."

"It's hard to figure guys out," Penny said. "Did you forward Ashley's 'true love' e-mail to her? Maybe it would have helped."

Oh. Yeah. I had forgotten all about it, and now the twenty-four hours had come and gone. I tried to veer the conversation in another direction. "I've been studying guys' body language lately. Have you ever noticed that if they lean toward you with their arms crossed, they're interested and want to impress you but are not committing?"

Penny grinned, leaped up, and grabbed a piece of her art paper. She sketched a guy in that pose. "Like this?"

I laughed. "Exactly! And if they sit with their toes pointing inward toward each other, then they're insecure."

Penny quickly inked another boy, this one looking just like a kid in my literature class.

"So what does a guy look like if he's just about to kiss you?" I asked.

"Personal research?"

I admitted it was. "I'm going to be sixteen in a month. You know, sweet sixteen and never been kissed." I sighed heavily to dramatize the moment, but she smiled softly at me. She knew it bugged me, and she knew how I hoped it would be remedied. And with whom.

Penny drew a boy leaning close, but not too close, looking both tentative and hopeful.

"Looks like Oliver," I teased her, and she blushed. "You know what? We should make a dude decoder for girls and e-mail it to our friends. I'll do the writing; you do the drawing."

She agreed, and as I called out my observations, she drew the sketches for each one.

DUDE DECODER

Stands with feet pointed inward:
Unsure of himself; he needs confirmation.

More than quick eye contact; lingering stare: **He's a player.**

Has his feet turned toward you in a crowd: **He's attracted to you.**

Crosses arms after rolling up sleeves: **He's trying to impress you by pushing forward his biceps.**

Keeps looking around after you start talking: **He doesn't like you; he's looking for an escape.**

Shows wounds or scars: **He's trying to impress with his manliness or get sympathy.**

We scanned the sketches and descriptions into the computer and sent them out to everyone we knew from Penny's e-mail, but signed with both our names.

"That was such a good idea," Penny said. "I haven't been able to use my art for much lately. I've got a friend, actually, who's getting ready to apply to art school. I've asked her if she'll work on an art project with me because I'd really like to learn from her."

I nodded slowly. Something about this was sounding familiar.

"I think we could both contribute to each other's projects—you know, working together, like you and I do. Plus, well, I could really use her help."

I swallowed hard. "Oh. What did she say?" My stomach was starting to feel sick. Too many cookies, probably.

"She's going to enter her portfolio for art school soon, and I think she wanted to do it on her own. But, well, I prayed about something for the first time ever. You know, like you do. And I think she might just work with me."

My chest felt heavy when she said, . . . *prayed* . . . *like you do."*

Because lately, I hadn't been.

In an instant I knew why this whole art scenario sounded familiar. It was last week's AFT column. Penny clearly hadn't read it, which was fine—it's not like she even knew I wrote it. And right now I was really glad she didn't know I wrote it. I could only hope that "Needs to Draw a Conclusion Soon" hadn't read it either.

Not likely.

Chapter 18

Tuesday morning I got to school really early because Melissa had said she'd help me a little bit with my writing and show me how to develop a sidebar. Since I didn't have my own desk, she let me sit at hers while she stood behind me and gave me tips. Suddenly Hazelle blustered over.

"It would make a lot more sense to move this—" she pointed over my shoulder at one of the paragraphs on the screen—"to the end. And we could delete this one—" she pointed at another one—"altogether."

Right. She could tell that by scanning it for like one minute?

She waited to see what I was going to do.

I wasn't going to do anything immediately, that was for sure. "Thanks," I said.

That must not have made her happy because she followed up with "Still trying to write about that dress shop, eh? We don't have a fashion column." Then she harrumphed to her desk.

I stared at the article. It bugged me to admit it, but Hazelle was right about moving the paragraph and deleting that other one too.

A few minutes later I got up to grab my bag and head toward first period. Melissa's desk was toward the back of the room, which gave me a good view of everything in sight. I stopped dead still and surveyed the boxing ring.

In one corner was the little cubby Natalie had taken over. A few bees buzzed around her sweet-smelling talk. I counted them. Six.

Then I looked over to the corner where Hazelle chewed on her pencil. A few people leaned over her desk, and a few others stood back listening and/or rolling their eyes. Six. Jack wouldn't vote. That left thirteen voting staff members, including me.

I wasn't in either circle right now. But I realized at that moment that I might well be the deciding vote. My stomach felt tender and vulnerable again, and I wondered if I could make it to the loo before maths.

Oooh. That Mrs. Simmons and her cookies.

Chapter 19

Wednesday night Dad dropped me off at church for coffeehouse and worship.

"Hey!" I tapped Supriya on the shoulder. "I'm sorry I didn't text you back last night. I fell asleep over my French book."

"No problem," she said. "I've already got my coffee. Do you want to get some, and I'll save you a seat?" She patted the crushed plush couch where we usually hung out and chatted before worship and the lesson.

I agreed and made my way to the barista cart. I was actually kind of glad because it gave me a chance to scan the room for Tommy without Supriya's teasing me. I carefully looked around, trying to appear like I was just casually taking in the scene, you know. As far as I could tell, he was nowhere to be found.

I had to admit I was a little disappointed. As I waited patiently and the people ahead of me got their drinks, I heard that still, small voice I hadn't heard as much lately as I used to.

Didn't you come here seeking Me?

Even though I knew it wasn't spoken aloud, I looked around to see if anyone else had heard it—the message was that strong. My head hung a little, and I apologized silently. As I did, a verse from VBS many summers ago came to me. As I thought about it, I promised to worship Him in spirit and truth. And I knew just how I could do that.

After I got my coffee I went over to talk with Supriya, and just before worship was about to begin, I found the youth pastor, Joe, and tapped him on the shoulder. I was going to tell him that I would be delighted to play guitar on the worship team.

"Oh, hey, Savvy," he said. "Have you prayed about the worship team yet?"

I stared at him. I'd promised myself, *no more little white lies.* And I certainly wasn't going to lie in church, about worship. Especially after I'd just told the Lord that I was going to worship in spirit and in truth.

"Uh, no." I could see the look of disappointment on his face. I felt disappointed too.

"Okay, then," he said. "We'd better get the show on the road." He headed to the stage, where he was joined by the keyboardist, the drummer, and one electric guitarist.

Halfway through worship, I realized that Joe hadn't said he was going to ask me again.

Chapter 20

Thursday afternoon I walked to Be@titude. It was warm, and I was wearing a new pair of white capris with a sporty tank layered over a tee. I had my big bag but not my notebook, as I was going for ministry purposes that night, not to take notes. The traffic was getting busy, so I looked twice to the right and the left before crossing the street. I really didn't want to have my obituary read, "Teen Girl Hit by Big Red Bus." That would be an embarrassing way to die.

I rounded the corner toward the shop and reached over to pluck a long-stemmed rose from a wild bush tumbling over an ancient stone wall. I thought about how old the village was. No one knows for sure, but some people think

Anne Boleyn, one of the wives of Henry VIII, was born in Kent. It was possible—not probable, but possible—that she'd been right in this area. Or at least could have seen it from the top of one of the castles.

I loved England.

I pushed the door to the shop open, pleased to see that there were two customers inside, one of them toting out a big, plastic-wrapped hanger bag. *Ka-ching!* More money for Becky.

"Hey, Savvy, I'm fairly busy," she said. "Do you want to thumb through some of those catalogs in the back for a few minutes till I can get you set up on the fund-raiser page?"

I nodded. Cool. I hadn't been able to look at them for myself last week, and I wasn't really in the mood to start up her expensive computer on my own. I went to the little office next to the try-on rooms and plopped down.

If I wasn't going to be a world-famous journalist, maybe I'd own a shop like this someday. I could picture it now. It'd be big, really big, and probably somewhere on Sloane Street, where all the fashionistas shopped. It'd have a big Dale Chihuly glass sculpture in the middle to acknowledge my American background. Everything would be sleek and modern. Including me. A lot of important people would shop there, probably Kate Middleton when she became princess. I'd have started my own ministry with the profits, and Princess Kate would find the idea fascinating and would want to put her royal stamp of approval on it. And then . . .

"Savvy!" Becky's voice popped through my daydream.

I blinked and looked at her. "Oh yeah."

"Are you okay?" She looked concerned. "I called you twice."

I nodded. "Just daydreaming."

She glanced at the stack of catalogs next to me. "Didn't get to look at any yet?"

I shook my head.

"Well, then, slip them into your bag, and you can look at them at home. I've got a lot of inputting for you to do, and then we'll be ready to send out the final auction announcement!"

She leaned over me to start up the computer, and I could breathe her perfume, something light and modern. Green but not floral. "Here's the list of people we need to add to the list." She tapped a yellow notepad. "And here are the other items we need to include on the auction page, which I'll just load now." She made a few clicks. "You're set! I'm going back to the shop to attend the clients and get a few other odds and ends done."

As she returned to the main room, I glanced up at the corkboard next to her computer station. There were snapshots on it of women, some with their kids. The women's names were under the pictures. There was a little date scribbled next to each picture—the date they'd first contacted Becky—for help, maybe?

I saw Isobel Alderman, with gap-toothed Emma standing right beside her. She had "21 April" scribbled beside her name. Not too long ago! Emma smiled down on me. I smiled at her picture and began to type.

Thirty minutes later I was finished! I snuck out into the store and stood behind Becky till I caught her eye. "All done," I said. "Everything is uploaded. You should be hearing from bidders tonight!"

"Nicely done, Savvy," she whispered. "I'll be with you in a minute." Then she turned again to help a shopper.

I moseyed back to the computer and sat down to wait. I looked at the Internet icon. Might as well check my e-mail. I logged on to the server and scrolled through a few.

A lot of Asking for Trouble forwards from Jack. I'd have to pick a question to answer soon. My heart buckled a little as I thought about my answer last week to the artist—the one Penny knew.

A forward about the garden club from my mom.

An e-mail from Natalie. Interesting. I clicked that one open and scanned the CC field. She'd sent it to everyone on the newspaper staff, talking about her plans for the next year. Should she win, that is.

And right before my eyes, a new e-mail arrived from . . . *"Your friend Ashley Gorm Strauss"?*

I clicked on that one too. It was an e-card. How nice! And it even had a benefit. It was from World Rice Bowl and promised to donate £1 toward world hunger for each person who opened the card. The sender would be notified about how much her *friends* had raised for her, as well as all the friends her friends forwarded it on to.

I looked out to the shop floor. Becky was still

chatting. I looked at the e-mail again. Surely it hadn't escaped *my friend Ashley Gorm Strauss* that I hadn't responded to her last forward about the true love of my life. Might as well open the card.

I clicked on the card icon, and as I did, I noticed by the bar on the bottom of the screen that it was downloading.

Wait a minute. I'd only meant to open the card. Not to download it onto Becky's computer.

I pounded the Escape button hard. Nothing. I hit Control-Alt-Delete. Nothing.

Becky was now ringing up the sale. It wasn't like I could shout for her.

All of a sudden the computer flashed twice, on and off, on and off. Then I noticed that my address book from my still-open e-mail account appeared on the screen, and the names and e-mail addresses began to scroll through. I tried to close out of the e-mail program, but it wouldn't shut down.

Desperate, I turned off the computer. My face was flaming hot. I could barely breathe. I was about to have my very first asthma attack; I was sure of it. Or heart attack, maybe.

The customer left the store, and Becky came

back. She took one look at my face and said quietly, "Savvy, what's wrong?"

Chapter 21

"Becky, I'm afraid I made a very big mistake."

Becky cocked her head but said nothing, nodding for me to continue but looking at the black computer.

"I sent everything out like you asked me to. And I got the site uploaded. But . . . well, when I was waiting here for you, I started reading my e-mail. Then I clicked on an e-card, and all of a sudden something started downloading." I told her the rest of the scenario, and as I did, her face went milky.

"Malware," she said.

Worst. Day. Ever.

Chapter 22

I offered to stay and help, but Becky said no, she'd better close the shop and figure out what happened. For all she knew, the malware had been sent to all the people on the donor list, and as soon as they opened the message from her, right after the e-mail announcing the auction, they would infect their own computers.

I gathered up my bag and the rest of my things. She said she'd contact me later but she'd really better get to figuring this out. My eyes felt like fireballs, and I barely made it out of the shop without crying. I lost it as soon as I heard her lock the door behind me . . . an hour early.

Lord, I prayed, holding loud, clamoring sobs inside through sheer willpower, *please, please,*

please don't let that e-mail have gone out to the donors. Please let this be a simple fix for Becky's computer. I'm so sorry that I made this mistake, Jesus. Just don't let a lot of those other people be harmed. Please, please, please.

I stopped pleading as I felt my phone vibrate, indicating an incoming text. It was from Penny.

Savvy. Don't open any e-mails from Ashley. Will explain more later.

Too late.

I walked a bit slower, hoping the cool air would calm down the red I knew must be splotching across my face. I pulled myself together, turned down Cinnamon Street, and headed to Kew Cottage. I could handle this. I could be calm.

I opened the door, and Growl came running toward me, but somehow he must have sensed something was wrong. He skidded to a stop, surfing on the small rug in the hallway.

Louanne came after him. "Sav . . ."

Before she could even finish my name, I raced upstairs into my room, slammed the door behind me, and let the sobs loose.

A minute later my mother knocked on the door. I didn't answer, but I didn't tell her to go away, either. She turned the knob and came in. For a few minutes she just sat and rubbed my back. In spite of myself, I was soothed. She said nothing, but I finally did.

"I ruined Becky's computer," I said. "With malware, whatever that is." Then I sat straight up in bed, remembering Becky's computer scrolling through my e-mail address book before I shut it down. "Mom! Did you get a message from me?"

"Well, I don't know, honey," she said in her quiet, calm tone, which indicated she seriously did not get the panic required by this situation.

"Mom, this is important." I bolted out of bed and ran downstairs. Dad was hunched over the computer, as he often was at night. "Dad, please log on to your e-mail right now and see if you got something from me."

He looked up at me and opened his mouth as if to say he was busy, but noticing my streaky face and watery eyes, he closed out of his program and logged on to his e-mail. "Nothing. Did you send it today?"

I took my first little breath of relief. "Can you log on to Mom's?"

He did. "Nothing."

He let me check my own e-mail. I quickly

clicked on my sent mail. Nothing had been sent that day. I deleted the message from Ashley, then permanently deleted it, and then I slumped on the couch and texted Penny.

Did you get an e-mail from me?

No. Did you open Ashley's card?

Yes.

A minute went by.

I'm so sorry, Savvy. Is your computer ruined? Two of Ashley's friends' computers are totally gone. Smoke. And they forwarded it to other people before it was too late.

I opened it at Be@titude.

I'm so, so sorry, Sav.

I didn't text back. Instead I quietly asked my dad, "What is malware?"

"*Malware* means '*mal*icious soft*ware*,'" he said. "Programs designed to cause a lot of damage. Why?"

I started crying again, and he came and sat next to me on the couch. I had to fight two desires at once. One, to let him hug me like he had when I was a little girl, and the other, to push him away and try to deal with this on my own. I bridged the difference and just drew a little closer and explained what had happened at Be@titude.

"Probably a computer virus, which is kind of like a Trojan horse. It looks like you didn't send it on after all because Mom and I didn't get an e-mail, and neither did Penny. Chances are good that if it would have gone to anyone on your list, it would have gone to everyone on your list."

"I didn't have time to pass on the forward," I said. Mom came down the stairs then, but to her credit, she said nothing about how she'd already told me that forwards were bad news. I stood up. "I'm going to bed now, I think," I said.

"At six o'clock?" Mom asked.

"I'm not hungry." All I could think about was that maybe Becky's address book had still been open after I entered the new e-mail addresses, and maybe the malware or Trojan horse or whatever it was had gone galloping into their computers too.

Once upstairs, I sat on my floor. I pulled out my laptop, but I didn't have the energy to do any work. Instead, I logged on to a Web site that would help me figure out what a Trojan horse was.

TROJAN HORSE

After many years of trying to conquer the city of Troy, the Greeks cunningly built a huge figure of a horse, inside of which a select force of fighting men hid. The Greeks pretended to sail away, and the Trojans pulled the horse into their city as a victory trophy, believing it to be a gift that would bring good fortune. That night, while the Trojans were distracted, the Greek force crept out of the horse and opened the gates for the rest of the Greek army, which had sailed back under the cover of night. The Greek army entered and destroyed the city of Troy.

I calmly logged off.

Yes, that's exactly what those forwards were. They promised something good to fake you out and let them in the computer "door." But once you opened them up and allowed them inside, they let loose all sorts of evil that not only didn't do good but destroyed all the good inside.

And then I realized, with a still, small nudge to my heart, that relying on lucky forwards and horoscopes and e-promises was exactly the same thing. A Trojan horse to my faith. I'd started relying on everything and everyone else—except God—to do the good I wanted.

I decided to read the real, actual Bible that night, not the one online. I opened up the one I brought to church, and the flyer I'd slipped in a few weeks back fell out. I read it carefully. I looked up the Bible verse.

Then I made a decision.

It was time to pray. I wasn't going to stop till I really knew I'd heard from God before telling anyone else.

Chapter 23

Sunday at church I worshiped in an amazing way. I learned more about the Lord and was able to honor Him with words both sung out loud and said in my heart. In Sunday school I had a great time with Supriya. Tommy came up to me and told me that I looked great. I think I glowed from the inside out.

My turning point was just around the corner. I felt it. I hoped I would hear it in prayer. But I still kept hearing, *Wait, wait, wait.*

I was waiting to hear . . .

Go!

Chapter 24

Monday night I started working on my column. I thought I should begin by looking up the verses I'd used for the last two columns. I wanted to jot them down in the notebook I used to keep track of the questions I'd answered so I didn't do too many with the same theme. I flipped to the last article where I'd used "God helps those who help themselves." I thumbed through my concordance.

Nothing. *Nothing?*

So I went to the one before that, where I'd used "God works in mysterious ways."

Thankfully, I found it: Isaiah 45:15. So one out of two wasn't bad, right? But it struck me then that while God does work in ways we don't always understand, He never works in ways that aren't true to Himself. That's what depending on luck or chance would be—putting my trust in good fortune and not in a good God.

I quickly looked up the other phrase online and instead was directed to a site full of quotes that people think are in the Bible but actually aren't. Deep sigh.

"Lord, I'm sorry."

"I am the vine; you are the branches. Those who remain in me, and I in them, will produce much fruit. For apart from me you can do nothing."

I knew that now.

I flipped through my Bible and finally settled on Ecclesiastes 4:9-10 as a response to this week's question. And for an uber-cool coincidence, one of the lines from that passage was also nearly the name of a Taylor Swift song: "Two Is Better Than One."

Dear Asking for Trouble,
Last year I had a problem. I felt like I was, you know, heavier than the other girls. Not fat. Maybe fat. Depends on who you ask. Anyway, I mostly took care of the problem by making myself ill after eating. I

dropped over a stone, and people noticed and complimented me. It felt good. Lately, well, I'm feeling a bit chubbers again. And sometimes there's that temptation to make myself ill like I did before. Part of me says it's all right to do it once in a while. The other part says, well, no, it's not. I can't tell anyone else about this problem, as you can well understand. What's your advice?

Sincerely,
Walking a Slim Line

♡

Dear Slim,
First, I want to compliment you for recognizing that you have a problem. If it weren't a problem, you wouldn't be writing in, right? But you are much stronger than most other people because you can see what you're doing wrong. I have to admit that I have made an error. Two weeks ago, in this column, I advised an art student to go it alone. Sketchy advice. I now realize that going it alone is not a good way to

operate, and I'm sorry I suggested it. We all need to help others. And we need those wiser than ourselves to show us the way. Please find the courage to visit the school counselor or talk with your mother, an aunt, or a minister. You can overcome this problem for good in a way that won't make you ill . . . or worse.

Healthfully Yours,
Asking for Trouble

Chapter 25

Monday I'd sat with the newspaper staff at lunch, but by Tuesday I was back sitting with Penny and the rest of the Aristocats. I nibbled on the meager offerings in my little plastic bag of chopped cucumbers with vinegar sprinkled over them and got my PowerBar out for after.

"My parents had to buy a new computer," Chloe said to the girl sitting next to her. "And it cost nearly a thousand pounds. They weren't too happy."

I didn't notice who gasped out loud because I was peeling back my PowerBar wrapper, but the rest of us all did the same in our heads. The table went dead quiet.

Ashley gave Chloe a look that could have

jellied Natalie and, without turning her gaze at all, finally said, "Well, these things happen." She brushed a few crumbs off the table, then turned to the left to begin a conversation with Alison, indicating that her "apology" had been offered and we shouldn't expect any more.

On the way out of lunch, I grumbled, "Was she dropped on her head at birth or something?"

Penny laughed out loud. "Oh, Savvy, you're so funny. Ashley is never going to say she's sorry. It's not her way."

"Can't say I feel terrible about Chloe's computer," I said. "But what about Becky's?"

"What happened to hers? Did you ever ask?"

"No, but I'll have to soon. I've already apologized. I'll have to do it again."

Penny gave me a hug. "That's the difference between you and Ashley, Sav."

"Well, and then there's the chauffeur-driven car, the multimillion-pound estate, the wardrobe closet the size of my house . . ."

"Well, that too," Penny teased. "Film this weekend?"

"I might have plans. And, uh, I might want to invite you. Busy on Saturday?"

"Nope," she said. "What's on?"

"Not sure," I admitted, trying to dodge her bewildered gaze. "I'll let you know tomorrow night."

♡

Later that afternoon I got home and found my mother tweaking her baskets and flowerpots in front of the house. "What are those?" I asked, more out of affection for my mom than interest in the names of the plants.

"Bacopa. They look nice with the red geraniums. I'm going to put some blue ones in here too. The baskets will be red, white, and blue. Just like both the American and British flags."

"Nice."

She followed me into the kitchen, chatting about her day. I offered her a Coke from the fridge, and as we drank them together, I looked out over the back garden area, bare and black since Aunt Maude, Louanne, and I had cleaned it up in April. "Why don't you plant some stuff out there?"

Mom shrugged. "Oh, I will. Waiting on the finances is all." Then she smiled and smoothed a hand over my hair. "Speaking of finances, have you heard anything from Becky?"

I shook my head. "It's been five days. Should I call her?"

Mom nodded. "I think it would be nice." She looked at me. "But difficult. Do you want to pray with me about it first?"

"Sure."

She set down her Coke can and enfolded my hands in her own before praying for peace and wisdom and a good conclusion. Then I went upstairs to make the call in private.

Chapter 26

I dialed the number and heard the quick, old-fashioned *ring-ring* of the British landline. Within two rings it was picked up.

"Good afternoon; Be@titude."

It was Becky.

"Uh, hi, Becky, it's Savvy." I held my breath, half expecting her to hang up. But she was acting out of her character as a person, not according to the situation.

"Hullo, Savvy," she said. "How was your weekend?"

"Very good," I said. "Thanks for asking. How was the auction? Were you able to get orders on the computer?"

"I took lots of bids on my home computer," she said.

"So . . . the computer at the store is being fixed?"

"It's being replaced," she said. "But I made just enough profit from the auction to cover the cost of a new system. It should be here next week."

"Oh." She didn't say it, but she didn't have to. The profits from the auction were being used to replace the computer, which meant they weren't being used to help fund the business wardrobes for the ministry.

"There's a little left over to help a few of the mums." She was trying to be encouraging. "And there's always the next fund-raiser. Thankfully, none of the donors' computers were affected."

Thank You, Lord.

"Is there anything else I can do?" I asked. *Haven't you done enough?* I scolded myself.

"Not just now," she said. "Do let me know if the shop write-up gets into the newspaper, though, okay? I'd love to have a clipping."

"Okay," I said. "Till then."

When I hung up, I had made yet another decision that I had to keep to myself. I was going to cast my deciding vote for whoever would promise to publish the article on Be@titude. It was the least I could do.

Chapter 27

After hanging up the phone, I went downstairs. As soon as I hit the landing, Louanne came skidding across the wood floor and grabbed my arm. "Can you take me to James Park? They're having a dog show trial. Mom is off to the book club, and I can't go alone."

Unfortunately, during my research the other day, I'd discovered that "It is more blessed to give than to receive" really *is* in the Bible. So it was something I needed to pay attention to even if I didn't always feel like it. "All right," I said.

"All right? As in yes?"

"As in yes," I said.

"Yahoo!" She slipped the collar around Growl's

neck. By the way he reacted, you'd have thought she was slipping a noose on him instead. He wriggled and yapped and twisted on the floor, trying to work it off.

"Better mellow out," I warned him. "It won't be a pleasant walk home for either of us if you don't qualify." I swore that dog could understand English. He chilled right out, and I was sure he winked at me.

Great. The dog was winking at me now, but still no guy was.

"I'm going to touch up my makeup and then we can go," I said.

"Why? You don't know anyone there. Who's going to see you? I'm going to be late!"

I ignored her and went to redraw my eyeliner and rebrush my hair. She was too young to realize that it didn't matter if you knew the people who saw you. People saw you.

We stepped out into the warm afternoon. A couple of blocks to the west of the village square was James Park, which was square too. I told Louanne I'd sit on a bench and wait for her, keeping my eyes on her, of course, but with my earbuds in, listening to my music. So I was startled when I felt a tap on my shoulder a few minutes later. I nearly jumped out of my skin. "Oh, uh, hi, Tommy." I took out the earbuds.

"Hey, Sav," he said. I kind of liked that he'd shortened my name. It made us seem . . . closer.

But I didn't want to shorten his. *Tommy* seemed so, well, boyish and British. "Hey. What are you doing here?"

He pointed across the field. "My gran brought her dog for the trial."

How could I forget this important detail about the very first time we'd locked eyes? Or maybe the second!

"You?" he asked.

"My sister has her dog trying out too."

"So . . . are you going to church tomorrow night?" Tommy asked. "We don't have practice, so I'm going to drop by."

The sun began to melt into the horizon, dappling the leaves on the apple trees around us as the branches bounced and swayed. Tiny blossoms began to push their way out of the fisted buds that constrained them—promises of fruit to come. A few of their misty petals landed on us as the wind whispered again. I felt peace in my heart about sharing my thoughts with Tommy, who was, at the end of the day, a brother in Christ even if nothing else. Yet.

"I'll be there," I said. "I've got a big decision to make before I go."

Tommy nodded.

"And I messed up one, or actually two, of my Asking for Trouble columns."

I knew he read all of my columns, and since he didn't disagree with my assessment, I figured he agreed with me. "Everyone makes mistakes, Savvy."

"I hadn't been searching in the right place for the answers," I said. "For direction. It was a good lesson."

He stretched, and when he was done, he ended up a few inches closer to me. "What kind of direction?"

"I'm going to look up the Bible verses from our Wednesday night groups over the past few months. And pray. And then wait to hear, 'Go.'"

He opened his mouth as if he was going to ask what I meant, but as he did, a tidy and pretty older-looking woman walked toward us. "Gran," he said, sounding both pleased and disappointed at her approach.

"Well, then, I wondered where I'd find you."

Her little Yorkie tugged on the leash toward me. The dog came closer and I petted him/her/it and smiled and made nice noises. It wasn't the first time—or the last time—I'd have to fake liking dogs for political reasons. "Who's your friend, Thomas?" Gran asked.

Thomas! Hee-hee.

He stood up, ready to ditch before we got a full-on BBC Channel 4 interview from Gran. But of course he answered her. "Her name is Savannah Smith."

"Pleased to meet you," I said, standing and holding out my hand.

"American, eh?" she said, noticing the accent I thought I'd very nearly erased.

"Yes," I said.

"Ah, the newspaper writer, right?"

I glanced at Tommy. Had he spilled my secret? He shrugged. I could tell by the look on his face that he was as shocked as I was.

How did she know?

"Yes," I answered honestly.

"Well, then, best be going," she said. "Might have a few sprinkles later on, and I've already had my hair done this week."

At that, Louanne ran up with a happy

expression on her face—Growl must have quali-
fied in spite of the odds—and I didn't want *her*
to know I wrote the column. So I was left silent,
wondering. How, and what, did Tommy's gran
know?

Louanne and I headed east, and Tommy and
his gran went west. As we walked away, he texted
me.

I swear, Savvy, I have never even mentioned you
to Gran before.

No problem.

As I typed it, I wasn't sure if the fact that he'd
never mentioned me before made me happy
or sad.

I put my phone away, and Louanne tugged my
arm. "Savvy, look who's in the village square."

Chapter 28

Right then I had two options—to take a turn and pretend I'd never seen them or to keep walking straight and bump into them. I would have liked to say I was courageous enough to walk straight on no matter what, but at that moment I was feeling pretty weak in the knees. But Louanne was with me, and she was heading straight, so I didn't have much of a choice.

Plus, Growl was not about to let us veer off course.

"Savvy! Louanne! Giggle!" Emma Alderman came racing toward us. She smiled brightly at Louanne and me and then dropped to her knees and rubbed Growl behind his scruffy little ears.

Isobel came along behind her and smiled at

me. Her face was lovely but still tired. The thought occurred to me that maybe being tired was a permanent condition for her.

"Hullo, Savvy," she said. "How goes the newspaper business?"

"Oh yeah, the newspaper!" Emma said. "Is my picture in it yet? Wait. You haven't even taken a snap of me yet."

Louanne nudged me and whispered, "Phone."

I looked at her, not making out what she was saying.

"Aketay the icturepay with the onephay," she said in pig latin. I supposed she was trying to keep Emma from understanding, but for a few seconds it kept me from understanding too.

"Oh, right," I said. "Yes, Emma, you're exactly, dead-on right. Here. You stand with your mum, and I'll take the snap with my phone camera. It's really very good."

It pained me, as a photographer, to say that.

"Oh no, not me," Isobel said.

"Yes, you too." I snapped a picture of the two of them grinning broadly in the fading daylight.

"Did you hear about Be@titude, then?" Isobel asked me.

"What do you mean?" I answered warily.

"Well, Becky had some kind of computer disaster. She had to replace her whole system. So the clothing program is off for a bit. Perhaps till September. We should pray for her." Isobel made no mention of her own setback, though she would now be getting no new clothes for job interviews.

"Yes, we should pray," I answered softly. Of course Isobel didn't know who had caused the problem. I felt confident Becky would never have told anyone else I was to blame for the malware meltdown.

"Well, we'd best be off," Isobel said.

"We actually get to eat supper out tonight. Though Mum says it has to be cheap and cheerful and not a posh nosh." Emma giggled at that, and we laughed along with her. "Be sure to tell me when I'm in the paper."

"I will," I promised as we left. "Oodgay anplay," I said to Louanne and was gratified to see that it took her some time to figure out what I was saying.

"So is she really going to be in the paper?" Louanne asked.

"Depends on if the new editor runs the article," I said.

"When's the election?"
"Next week."

Chapter 29

After midnight that night, I snuck down into the living room—er, lounge. The draperies were pulled open, and the moonlight lit the room in a magical way, like a fine mist over everything. I settled on the couch and curled my feet up under me and opened my Bible. Then I pulled out the piece of paper from Wednesday night. I read John 15:5 and thought about the branches blowing in the park. I thought about the sweet-smelling blossoms that promised ripe fruit.

In my Bible, I found another paper Joe had handed out at church recently. I looked up the verse from the bottom of the page.

Jesus explained, "I tell you the truth, the Son can do nothing by himself. He does only what he sees the Father doing. Whatever the Father does, the Son also does. For the Father loves the Son and shows him everything he is doing."

My real problem was that I had done what *Savvy* wanted to do without asking the Lord if that was what *He* wanted me to do. My desire was to do ministry. I didn't ask Him what ministry He desired for me to do.

My dad had shown me how he'd protected our computer from malware. First, you needed a program that would identify anything bad that wanted to get into your system. The computer had to recognize something was wrong—Trojan horse or not—and stop it at the door.

I grinned and looked down at my Bible. Check.

Second, if something did get through, you had to remove it right away. Acting fast was the key to minimizing damage.

Repentance.

Lord, I'm so sorry I ran ahead of You. I do love You. I want to do good things. But I only want to do the good things You prepared in advance for me to do.

So help me to remain connected to You and do what I see that You want me to do.

And then, in the quiet of the night, I heard it. It was in my heart, but it was loud and unmistakable.

Go!

Chapter 30

On Wednesday night I got to church early. They hadn't even set up the coffee stand yet. I found Joe and waited patiently while he finished talking to another staff member.

"Hullo, Savvy. What can I do for you?"

"I want to be baptized next Saturday."

"Are you sure?" he asked.

"Very sure," I said.

Joe grinned. "Well, then, let's talk!"

Chapter 31

It was the second Saturday in June, so it was supposed to be warm, right? summerish? Not quite! Although I was grateful it wasn't raining, it was definitely not beach weather. I had a big towel in my bag, though. We were going to pick Penny up and then head out of town to a private bank on the River Thames.

Mom, Dad, Louanne, and I piled into the car and pulled out of the drive. Vivienne, our next-door neighbor and Mom's book club friend, gave us a cheery wave as she plucked dead leaves from the plants on her porch. She'd come by last night to ask Mom about the library guild meeting. Mom had said she couldn't go because I was going to be baptized.

"Didn't get it done as a baby, then?" she'd said to me. "Shame, that."

I had tried to give it another shot myself, saying it wasn't an oversight that I hadn't been baptized yet, but an intentional decision. "I wanted to wait until I was old enough to make my own decision to follow Christ. I wanted to choose this for myself and know what I was signing up for."

Vivienne had still shaken her head. But she'd brought over a pack of hot cross buns this morning, and this being months after Easter, I thought she meant something special by that. I gave her an extra-toothy smile as we drove away.

"I heard there are still lots of eels in the River Thames," Louanne shared.

"You sure know how to put a person at ease," I said.

"Just saying." She sounded older than her ten years. Then we both burst out laughing.

When we pulled in front of Hill House, Penny was waiting. I felt almost as nervous about having Penny come as I did about sharing my testimony in front of everyone who was going to be there. What would she think? That we were religious nut cakes? Shame that I wasn't baptized as a baby?

I hoped she wouldn't rethink our friendship. I didn't want her to think our car was a clunker compared to her sports car. We five were going to be squeezed as tight as a stack of jam butties in cling wrap once she piled into the Ford too.

"Hey, Savvy," Penny said as I opened the door and scooted over. She grinned at me, same as always, and I felt my heart relax.

Once we got to the park, we piled out of the car and went down to the riverbank, which looked like hardened brown sugar with a crumbling edge. I saw Joe down there, wearing a pair of plaid shorts and a polo shirt, his wife and their new baby next to him. I recognized a couple of other people from the class we'd gone to in preparation for this. Their families were there too.

And so was Supriya!

"Hey, what are you doing here?" I gave her a big hug.

"I wouldn't miss it for anything." She leaned over and, even before being introduced, hugged Penny. "You must be the famous Penny. Savvy told me you were coming."

"She just didn't tell me *you* would be here!"

Penny responded, but I could tell she was pleased to have been mentioned at all.

Supriya nudged me. "Have a look over there."

Coming down the hill from the parking lot was Tommy.

Chapter 32

He was in his soccer—um, football uniform. "I didn't know he was going to show up," Penny said.

"I didn't know either," I whispered. Then I spoke up, trying to appear unfazed. "Hey, Tommy!"

He came over and gave me a friendly hug. It was the first time he'd ever done so, and even though guys and girls hugged each other all the time at school, this time I was very aware that my dad was only feet away, watching the whole thing.

"Hey, Sav," he said. "I hope it's okay . . ."

I grinned. "I'm so glad you could come. But your match?"

"I'll be a little late," he said. "My grandfather

is waiting in the car to take me to the game in a bit." I'd forgotten that Tommy's mom had broken her foot and couldn't drive yet, and his dad often traveled for work.

"Thank you," I said softly.

"Not at all," he answered. And then it was time for me to head down to the riverbank.

I wasn't sure, but I guessed that the River Jordan, where Jesus was baptized, was a bit warmer than the River Thames. Oh, and by the way, it probably didn't have eels. But I still thought it was cool to be baptized in a river, just like Jesus.

Two people went ahead of me, and then it was my turn to face the group of people gathered. I shared how I had become a Christian when I was a little girl. And also how I kept forgetting whether I'd really asked Jesus to be the Lord of my life, so my mom had told me I should go ahead and give my life to Him once more and she'd write the date on the back of a wooden cross. We hung the cross in my bedroom and then, anytime I wondered if I was really His, I'd pull the cross off my wall and look at it, reassured.

Then I mentioned the forwards and texts. "Some of those texts and e-mails promised good things. But every good thing comes only from God. They also threatened disaster if I didn't 'obey' them. But the only time I was flirting with disaster was when I trusted them. I don't believe in luck. Or chance. Or horoscopes. I trust God. That's all."

I smiled and indicated to Joe that I was ready.

Chapter 33

Joe waded into the flat brown water with me, my flip-flops suctioning for all their worth in the silty riverbed. Once we were a few feet out, he said loudly enough for everyone on the bank to hear, "Based on your profession of faith and your desire to follow Christ wherever He leads you, I baptize you, Savannah Smith, in the name of the Father, the Son, and the Holy Spirit."

I closed my eyes as he put his arm around me, but it didn't feel like Joe's arm—it somehow felt like God's. He was holding on to me, and there was nothing that could separate me from Him.

"Two are better than one."

When Joe lifted me out of the water, everyone

on the shore clapped, and I made my way to the edge. My mom held out a towel and dried off my face before handing it to me to wrap up in.

A few others were baptized. Tommy gave me a little wave good-bye and then slipped silently up the bank again to the parking lot, where his grandfather waited to take him to his game.

My mom pulled me aside and handed me a jewelry box.

"What's this?" I asked.

"Open it," she said.

Dad and Louanne came alongside me too; Penny and Supriya were talking with some of the others. Out of the corner of my eye, I could see Supriya introducing Penny to them.

I turned my attention back to the jewelry box and cracked it open. The hinges moved smoothly. Inside was a beautiful gold cross.

"Turn it over!" Louanne said.

I did. On the other side was etched today's date—making a matching set, in a way, with the cross on my wall. "Thank you," I said and kissed each of their cheeks. "I'm kinda cold. I might go see if Penny is ready to go." They said they'd meet us at the car.

I walked up to Supriya and Penny. "Hey!"

"That was lovely," Penny said. "I've never seen anything like it."

"Thank you," I said.

"I have a gift for you, Savvy," Supriya said, "but it's not something I can hand to you."

I cocked my head to the side. "Well, thank you. But what is it?"

"I know the problems you've had with the forwards and the texts and all. And, you know, I've been tempted by them myself. So each week I'm going to find a Bible verse and text it to you. That'll be the encouraging text for the week instead. You can even forward it, if you want."

At that, the three of us started laughing. We said good-bye, and Penny whispered, "You know, Savvy, I wouldn't mind if you forwarded it on to me."

"I will," I said, seeing the possibility of a new branch shooting from the Vine.

"Savvy, can I see you for a second?" Joe called, waving me over.

I nodded and asked Penny if it would be okay if she went to the car ahead of me.

"Nicely done," Joe said. "Have you prayed about playing on worship team?"

I smiled broadly. "I have—and I'd love to."

"Good." Joe turned to go, but then he stepped back toward me, a serious look suddenly replacing his grin. "I'll be sending you a packet of information via e-mail tonight or tomorrow, just some follow-up Scriptures and thoughts. You know, sometimes things actually get more difficult for a bit after baptism. I just want to warn you."

I looked at him, slightly alarmed. "What do you mean?"

"Well," he started, "it's like a new car."

Inwardly, I groaned. Was there no end to where *Top Gear* and speedy cars interrupted my life? But I said nothing, allowing him to continue.

"You do the design, you unveil the new model—and then you do several test-drives to see how it handles real-life challenges and where adjustments might need to be made."

"Tests?" I said. "Challenges?" That didn't sound like a slow country drive down safe, straight roads.

"Even the Lord was led into the desert for testing shortly after His baptism, Savvy," Joe said. "Testing will come. Probably right away."

Chapter 34

Supriya's first text came that night, right after I'd slipped on both my new cross and my pajamas. I was really excited to get the text, till I looked up the verses: Isaiah 43:1-3.

> *Do not be afraid, for I have ransomed you.*
> > *I have called you by name; you are mine.*
> *When you go through deep waters,*
> > *I will be with you.*
> *When you go through rivers of difficulty,*
> > *you will not drown.*
> *When you walk through the fire of oppression,*
> > *you will not be burned up;*
> > *the flames will not consume you.*
> *For I am the LORD, your God,*
> > *the Holy One of Israel, your Savior.*

I figured she'd picked that passage because I'd just been baptized in a river and the words had some similarities. But she had probably prayed about which verses to send too. Part of me felt encouraged. Part of me moaned, *But I don't want deep waters or rivers of difficulty or fires of oppression!*

Chapter 35

Sunday at church I met with the worship team. Everyone was welcoming, and I knew I was going to fit right in. I got the music for the next Wednesday and took it home to practice. I agreed to come early on Wednesday nights so we could go over the songs once or twice before hanging out.

So far, so good.

Then at Sunday school, Tommy pulled me aside. "Hey, are you interested in going to a film next Saturday?"

"Um, sure," I said.

"Oliver is asking Penny, and my friend Bill and his girlfriend, Maddie, are coming too."

I exercised amazing control over all forty-three of my facial muscles so I wouldn't smile. Three couples. It's not like we were official or anything, but these were definitely couples. And since it wasn't a one-on-one date, I knew my dad would let me go.

"I'd love to."

"Great." He grinned. "I'll get you the details later in the week."

If this was the testing, bring it on!

Chapter 36

Monday we stayed after school to have our final newspaper meeting before the Great Vote. We got to hear from each of the candidates. I personally thought it was a huge waste of time because everyone had already divvied up into Team Hazelle and Team Natalie.

Except for me, of course. Less than twenty-four hours before the vote, I was still wishy-washy. Natalie found me before the meeting was about to begin. "Almost finished with that article on Be@titude?" she asked. "I'm looking forward to seeing it. And hearing your ideas for a spirituality column."

I nodded and smiled, but she still made me feel like I needed to escape her as soon as possible. I supposed that didn't matter. You had to be able to work with and for people you didn't necessarily like. Especially if they were going to help you meet your goals. Christian goals that were going to help other people, too. Like Becky. And Emma.

Hazelle didn't try to sway me in any way. She wasn't even particularly friendly. She went about her business doing what she normally did with her hangdog, I-miss-Brian look whenever I caught her unawares. It was a good thing she was running for editor and not for public office because she seriously didn't know how to manage a campaign.

She did try to dress up her uniform a bit, though; I'd give her that. But then she had to go and ask my opinion.

She pulled me aside. "Savvy, what do you think of the accessories—makeup, hair, you know?"

I looked her over and offered nothing.

"Go ahead," she said. "I asked you because I can trust you to be honest with me. You've got a lot of shortcomings, but you're always honest."

A lot of shortcomings, eh?

"Well," I said. "Um, I think that, you know, you've got a lot of natural beauty that the heavy makeup is covering up. And there's a lot of humidity in England. Pretty much everyone's got to straighten their hair to keep away the frizzies." Her face looked so fragile that I reached for something kind but true to say. I glanced at her bracelets—cool Indian bangles like Supriya might wear. "Love the bracelets," I said.

"Thanks," she said. "I got them at the museum gift shop."

Her dad was a security guard for the British Museum. But there was girl rule #169: Don't tell people you bought your accessories at a museum. "They're beautiful," was all I said. And they were. Then I saw a look cross her face for the first time.

She was worried about the vote.

Chapter 37

Tuesday morning we cast our votes.

"Thanks, everybody," Jack said. "I'll take the votes and tally them. After I've had a chance to talk with both candidates, I'll make a general announcement."

At lunch Hazelle was not at the newspaper table, and neither was Jack. I sat with Penny because I couldn't stand the tension at the Wexburg Academy *Times* table.

I went home and did my homework, ate dinner, and turned in my column to Jack. This wouldn't normally be a column week for me, but he'd juggled the editorial schedule a bit to accommodate end-of-the-year events. Then I tried to sleep.

In first period on Wednesday, I knew the answer before Jack had even made the announcement. Hazelle flounced into first period, her Ruby Desire lipstick as dark as ever, and plopped down right next to me.

"Hey, Hazelle," I said.

She smiled at me, but it was a superior I-am-the-queen kind of smile. "Hullo, Savannah," she said.

"I take it congratulations are in order?" I said.

She nodded. "Yes, thanks."

"Oh, good," I said, my hopes starting to flail a little at her iceberg-just-below-the-surface attitude. "Maybe sometime this week we can talk about my article. Maybe Thursday, when the new edition of the paper comes out?"

"I'll try to squeeze it in," she said. "I'll have a lot going on during the transition. I'm sure we'll be able to give you some little topic to fulfill Jack's promise." And with that, she turned to what was, I assumed, a very important text before Mr. Thompson came in to start class.

I purposely avoided Brian so I wouldn't have to make eye contact with him. Before today, I'd been thinking he was a creep for dumping Hazelle. But now I wasn't so sure.

After class I saw Natalie in the hall. I tried to smile, but she glared at me and started to walk by. Then she turned on her heel and came after me. "You made a very bad choice," she said. "And it's all going to come down on your head. Wait and see." Then she threw her arm around Rhys's waist and strode away.

She knew I'd had the deciding vote and hadn't voted for her. I thought I'd done the right thing—even if Hazelle wasn't warm and fuzzy, at least she was trustworthy and honest. But what had Natalie meant about it all coming down on my head?

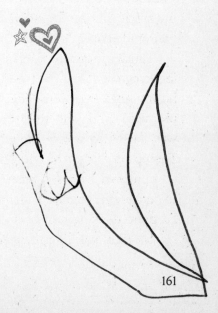

Chapter 38

Wednesday night, my first night with the worship team. I was kind of sad because neither Supriya nor Tommy was there, but it did allow me a chance to get to know the others in the worship band. For some reason, though, I had the sense that doom was just ahead. I couldn't shake the dark feeling. I was in the house of the Lord, playing His music with His people, and I still felt nervous.

It reminded me of a feeling I'd had when I was little. Once, in the middle of the night, I could hear noises coming from underneath my bed. I just had to lie there and hope that daylight would come soon. In the morning, Dad looked and said nothing had been there, but I knew different. Something had been after me.

Chapter 39

Thursday finally arrived, and my column was in the paper—the one I'd based on real Scripture again. Before I left to deliver the papers, I stopped Hazelle in the newspaper office. "Can we meet today?"

"Sure," she said, but I couldn't read her expression. "After school, in here, okay?"

"Okay." Maybe things weren't going to be so bad after all. She'd let me do the Be@titude piece, and we'd be okay. I let my mind turn to happier things—the group date with Tommy on Saturday night.

At lunch, Jack pulled me aside. "Savvy, I wanted to let you be the one to tell Hazelle the news that you were writing the Asking for Trouble column.

But when her sister found out Hazelle had made editor, she started discussing things with her, including your writing the column and how Julia had thought it was a brilliant idea."

"Oh," I said. "How did Hazelle take it?"

"Not well, I'm afraid. I won't be here after school today, as I've got a tennis match. But I wanted you to know."

To be warned, he meant.

After school I stepped into the Wexburg Academy *Times* office. One look at Hazelle's bright red face when she glanced in my direction slowed me right down. I heard the breathing under the bed again.

Something was very wrong. She pulled me into Jack's office and closed the door behind her. She sat down at Jack's desk, and I sat on the other side, like a kid in the headmaster's office. All I could think was, *You made this monster, Savvy. You voted her in.*

Yes, but after prayer. It was bewildering. Had I heard incorrectly?

"I'm really disappointed," Hazelle started. "I mean, well, I do see that you have some—or the beginnings of some—writing talent. But above all, I thought I could always trust you to be honest with me. And all this time you've been lying, kind of. Keeping the secret that you were the writer of the advice column. Julia told me that hadn't been a part of the deal. That it had been *your* idea." She drummed her fingers on the desk. "Why didn't you tell me?"

My own face was red now; I could feel it. Hazelle was calling me a liar when my motives had been pure. However, she was the new editor, and it was going to be up to her whether or not I wrote the story about Be@titude—and also whether or not I kept my column.

She was waiting for an answer, I could see. Here were some of the things I could have told her, all of them honest, though I had no idea if any of them would even wash with her:

1. We weren't friends then, and apparently we aren't really friends now, though I kind of thought we were. So why should I tell you anything?
2. Because I felt that God wanted me to do my good deeds in private, but you wouldn't understand because you think religion is for fruitcakes.
3. Because I didn't want to hurt your feelings

since I was chosen and not you. I knew
you'd feel bad that your sister didn't
pick you.
4. Because no one thought our school would
listen to an American.

Oh, all right. "Well, I didn't think anyone would
listen to an American. So I needed to build credi-
bility first."

She stared at me, but I could practically read
her thoughts: *Oh. Right. Makes sense, then.*

"Well, Savvy, journalistic integrity is critical.
Critical! I have to know what you're doing and
why and that you'll be honest with me and that I
can trust you to do what the paper needs."

"You can," I said. "Really."

Hazelle looked at me. "All right, then. Here's
an assignment for you. Up till now, Natalie
has been in charge of getting our horoscope
column delivered to us from one of the local
syndicates. She's decided to leave the paper
immediately."

What? Natalie was quitting?

"That means we need a new horoscope column. Whoever was supplying it to Natalie was
doing it for free as a courtesy to her. She's angry,

and she said she's going to put an end to that. That's where you step in. You need to keep the horoscope column going."

"But . . . how?" I asked.

"That's your problem to solve," Hazelle said. "Be resourceful. Ask Natalie who she was using. Find another source and get reprint permission. Or—" she snorted—"write it yourself. Seems easy enough to do. Like giving advice."

I could have closed in for the kill right then and told her that if just anyone could write them, they obviously weren't true. But I thought it might be better to hold that comment for another day.

Horoscopes. This was a test, all right. A test of my loyalty to her, to the paper. To my promise to God.

"I need the column by Monday night. You'll have no trouble making that deadline, I'm sure." She stood up. I was being dismissed.

"And what about my other work? the Asking for Trouble column? the article for the paper at the end of June?"

"I don't want to divert your attention away from this important task," she said. "So I'll just put those others on hold till we talk next week."

I turned to leave.

"Oh, Savvy? You can keep delivering the paper, though."

Chapter 40

Penny agreed to meet me at Fishcoteque for an emergency serving of fish, chips, and Fanta, even though she said she was feeling really tired.

"So what are you going to do?" she asked.

I shrugged. "I'm trapped. If I tell her I'm not going to do it, she's made it very clear she'll reassign my other work." I didn't come clean on exactly what that entailed, since my column was still mostly a secret. "My article for Be@titude will be killed."

"Killed?" Penny dipped a chip into some ketchup while she waited for me to reply.

I tucked one leg under the other to find a more comfortable position in the leatherette booth. "*Kill* is a term journalists use when an article has been assigned and then the editor cancels it."

"Why not use the term *cancel*?" She went for a second piece of fish.

"I dunno," I said.

Jeannie must have noticed my glum face when we walked in because she brought around another paper-wrapped cone of chips. "Here you are, luv. It's on me."

"Thank you, Jeannie," I said. Penny, of course, dove right in. "And then there are deadlines," I said. "Why do writers have to use the word *dead*? I mean, can't we just say due dates or something?"

"Makes sense to me." Penny sneezed. "Excuse me. Writing is a lot more violent than I ever thought."

Thinking back to Hazelle and Natalie, I had to agree.

"So why did you vote for her?" Penny asked.

"Two reasons. One, she is a good writer and editor. I felt like I could trust her, and well, I felt she would be the better person for the job."

"And the second reason?"

"I never really trusted Natalie. She made a lot of promises, but I never fully believed she'd come through."

"Hazelle might not either," Penny said. "But at least she didn't make promises. So . . . why not just ask Natalie for the name of the horoscope writer?"

"For starters, I doubt she'd give it to me. Besides, it seems like it was a friend who was doing her a favor. And maybe the biggest reason, I'm not going to arrange for horoscopes. They're malware."

Penny stopped eating and smiled. "That's the difference between you and Hazelle," she said.

"That and the fact that she's the editor of the paper and can write whatever and whenever she wants," I said.

"Well, yes, there's that, too," Penny said, sneezing again. "Sorry about that. Must be the vinegar. Well, you've got till Monday to figure it out. And we have Saturday to look forward to."

"True!" I said, fervently glad that there was one bright spot in my life.

Chapter 41

I awoke Saturday morning to a text from Penny.

> I'm not feeling so well this morning. I'll see how I'm doing as the day goes on, but just to make sure, Bill and Maddie are going, right?

> Let me check.

I glanced at my watch. Tommy would be leaving for football in like ten minutes. I speed-texted.

> Hey—good luck at the match today. Bill is still coming tonight, right?

Thanks. Bill is fine. Just talked to him—he's gearing up for the game. Better run. I'll see you about 7:30, right?

Big sigh of relief.

Yeah, see you then!

Four hours later, Penny texted.

Sorry, Sav. I still have a fever. Text me as soon as you get back and let me know all the details.

I spent the next hours doing my homework, finishing my chores, and trying on about eight outfits. After finally settling on my second-best skinny jeans with gold flip-flops and tank top layered with a peasant shirt, I decided I'd better do a pedicure. My polish was chipped; it looked like mice had been nibbling at my toe tips.

I checked my watch. Two hours to go. Plenty of time to do my hair.

I begged my mother to drive me on her way to a dinner with the ladies in her Bible study. "Please. It's embarrassing enough to be dropped off alone, now that Penny can't go." I loved Dad, but he was bound to do something mortifying. Thankfully, she agreed.

Wexburg didn't have its own movie theater, so we drove to the next village over. I hated arriving when no one else was there—you felt like such a loser hanging out in front of the theater alone. But Mom had insisted that we leave a bit early so she would still be able to get to her dinner on time.

So I stood outside the cinema and waited. I hoped Tommy would arrive before Bill and Maddie. He did!

"Hey!" He strolled up to me. It looked like he'd rubbed a little gel through his wavy brown hair, and his eyes were still as deep as dark chocolate. Lately we hadn't been turning away from direct eye contact; we'd been holding it instead. I know it's a cliché, and as a writer, I was supposed to avoid them like the plague, but my stomach really did do somersaults.

"Hi," I said. "How was the game?"

"We won!" His face was flushed with high spirits. "But Bill got hurt. Someone actually kicked him really hard in the shin. He's got to get it looked at, so he won't be able to come tonight. Funny about your asking if he was coming this morning. Where's Penny?"

"Sick," I said, starting to feel that way myself. "That's why I texted you to see about Bill earlier. So Maddie isn't coming either?"

"Nah. It'd be weird without Bill since you two aren't friends. I guess it's just the two of us then. Should I buy the tickets?"

Just the two of us. I'd have loved for him to have bought the tickets for "just the two of us." After all, I was nearly sixteen. I mean, come on. We were at a public movie theater. He was a Christian. But even though I was allowed to go out with people, my dad had said no one-on-one dates till I was sixteen.

Chapter 42

"I'm really sorry, but I don't think I can stay," I said.

He looked at me strangely. "Why not?"

I hated that I had to be the person to say that word *date* first, because we weren't even official. It's not like he had asked me to go out with him. "I'm not allowed to go anywhere, um, you know, one-on-one with anyone till I'm sixteen."

"One-on-one?" He still looked puzzled.

Okay, apparently I was going to have to do the heavy lifting here. "A date," I said. "My dad says I'm not allowed to date till next month."

Next month. It sounded so ridiculous and legalistic. Twenty-eight days.

"I could text my dad and ask him if it's okay," I said.

He shook his head. "That's all right. If that's his rule, we should respect it."

So I texted my dad—because my mom was at church—and asked him to come and pick me up. Tommy and I stood and made small talk, which was, surprisingly, not terribly uncomfortable, given the situation. We were even laughing when my dad pulled up. Tommy waved as I got in the car.

"Does he have a ride home?" Dad asked.

"I don't know."

"Well, ask him!"

I rolled down the window, feeling ridiculous all over again. "Do you have a ride?"

"I can hang out for a couple of hours till my dad gets home," he said. "My grandparents dropped me off on their way to dinner. My mom still can't drive because her cast isn't off her foot yet."

"My dad said we can give you a ride home."

I had to admit, I was totally shocked when he headed toward the back door and opened it. "Thanks!" he said.

I sat fairly silently as we drove to Tommy's house. He and my dad talked about football and cars and *Top Gear*. I let my mind wander because I didn't know a lot about cars. However, the thought occurred to me as I listened to them talk about test tracks that maybe tonight was one of the tests Joe had mentioned.

We soon got to his house. It was nice—a single home, not a semidetached like mine, but not a mansion like Hill House. As I looked over the beautiful front garden, I remembered that his mom was also in the garden club that Penny's mom and Ashley's mom were a part of. And that my mother still hadn't been voted in.

"Good night, Savvy," Tommy said as he got out. "And thank you for the ride, Mr. Smith."

"Not at all," Dad said. After Tommy got into his house, Dad turned to me and said, "He's a nice young man."

"Thanks."

"I'm proud of you for doing the right thing. Even if it doesn't always feel good or work out the way you hope it will."

Chapter 43

When I went to school on Monday, I felt all "prayed up," as my old Sunday school teacher would have said. Worship was great on Sunday, and then I spent some time with my family. All in all, I felt even closer to Tommy after our movie fiasco than if we had gone. It gave us something to laugh about together and harass our friends about for abandoning us.

He still hadn't officially asked me to go out with him, though.

Anyway, I was prepared for Hazelle—and our talk—on Monday. Or at least I thought I was. We'd agreed to meet after school. I sat with Penny at lunch, but when I turned around to look at the newspaper staff table, I noticed that Hazelle wasn't eating anything for lunch. I wasn't either.

After school I grabbed my stuff to head over to the office.

"Good luck," Penny said. "Text me when it's over."

The newspaper office was still pretty busy. Melissa and Jack had mainly cleared out their stuff, although Jack was there most days helping to transition Hazelle. Everyone else was hard at work writing or editing. Everyone except me, that is.

"Come on into my office," Hazelle said. I noticed how she rolled the words *my office* off her tongue with ease. She hadn't lost her bossy tone, but maybe there was a little less sting to it than the week before.

I sat down in the very chair I'd sat in when I was trying to convince Jack to let me write for the paper at the beginning of the school year. Here I was, nearly a year later, doing the exact same thing.

"So have you given any thought to the horoscope column?" Hazelle asked.

"Yes, I have. I take my writing and the Wexburg Academy *Times* very seriously. But in the end, Hazelle, I just can't do anything with the horoscopes. I'm sorry."

She looked shocked. "You're kidding."

"No, I'm not kidding. As committed as I am to this paper, I can't compromise my principles to write a column. What kind of advice giver would I be if I told everyone to give up what they believed in so they could get something they wanted, you know?"

"That's not what I've asked you to do," she said, defending herself.

"I understand that. But that's how I see it. I just can't do it."

"Well, then, I'm sorry, Savvy. I need someone who can do what the paper needs." She pulled her pencil from behind her ear and tapped it on the desk in front of her. I could hear her foot tapping underneath the desk.

I was nervous too, but I did my best to keep my feet—and my voice—steady. "Then I guess that's all there is to it," I said.

Hazelle stood and headed toward the office door. "I have to do what's best for the paper."

I joined her next to the still-closed door and made my final comment. "If that's true, you'd agreed with Jack that I could write an article.

It seems like journalistic integrity would apply there, too."

Hazelle looked like I'd slapped her. She flung open the door and walked out. I followed close behind her, bumping into Natalie as I did.

Natalie took one look at both of our flushed faces and then turned toward me. "I told you this would go badly. Too bad you never quite got over Rhys preferring me to you. If you had, you'd have voted for me and none of this would have happened."

"What do you mean?" Hazelle burst in.

"You're apparently not bright enough to realize that Savvy held the swing vote. I tallied up all those I could count on to support me before the election—it came to exactly six. And then I counted up your supporters. Six. Which left Savvy."

I stood between them again, knowing what Natalie said was true. I'd done the sum myself.

After dropping her little bomb, Natalie turned her back to us, took her heavy book bag—presumably packed with the last of the stuff she'd had at her Wexburg Academy *Times* desk—and flounced out.

Chapter 44

On Tuesday, Penny came home from school with me. We hung out in my room with crisps and dip and Coke. She pulled out a big old navy blue case. It definitely didn't look like the usual posh Penny fare.

"What's that?" I asked.

"My art portfolio," she said. "Battered and tatty as it may be." She unzipped it and took out a booklet. Then she handed it to me.

"The dude decoder!" I flipped through it. She'd taken our initial ramblings and sketches and made them into a real booklet. "So cool."

"I thought so too." She grinned. "I showed them to the girl I'd mentioned to you—remember, the one I wanted to share an art project with?

She thought it was awesome too—and she even said we could work together on our final project! Thanks for the idea."

We flipped through the pages and laughed over some of the drawings. I stopped at the page with the sketch of a guy about to kiss someone.

"Not ready to turn the page?" she teased.

I threw a pillow at her. "I'm studying the pose. Just so I'll know what I'm looking for."

A couple of hours later she headed home, and as I closed the door behind her, I said to my mom, "I feel kind of bad having her over here. I mean, her house is so big. And she has a housekeeper."

"We may not have a housekeeper, but we do have Aunt Maude," Mom replied, a wicked gleam in her eye. "She's coming on Thursday. For the night. Dad and I are going to spend the night in London for a work conference."

No. No. No. I would have enough trouble as it was this weekend, trying to decide if I should contact Becky again before writing the article, figuring out how to make the article exciting enough to generate buzz. I didn't need Aunt Maude on top of it all.

Chapter 45

Thursday after school I arrived to a house that smelled faintly like skunk.

"Hullo, dear," Aunt Maude said as I walked into the kitchen.

"Hello, Aunt Maude, how are you?" I asked politely, dreading her response. My dad was grinning behind his newspaper. I knew it, even though I couldn't see his face. I could see the paper quiver.

"I'm simply awful," Maude said. "My varicose veins are popping faster than a drug addict's. Do you want to see?"

She reached down and was ready to pull up a polyester pant leg when I hurriedly rushed in with "No, no thank you. Weak stomach."

"Well, all right, then," she said. "And then

189

there's the digestive system. My goodness. You've never heard so many noises. I never have, anyway. My friend Agnes told me that I'm right to be concerned and that she's going to arrange a visit with a specialist on Harley Street straightaway. So we'll be eating soft food tonight."

"Oh, yum. What are we having?" I leaped at the opportunity to change the subject.

"I'm making bubble and squeak right now," Maude answered.

I glanced over to where my father was sitting in the corner, reading his paper. The paper was absolutely shaking now. "Dad, can you come upstairs?" I asked.

"Sure, Savvy." He closed the paper, and I knew he was using all his self-control to hold those forty-three facial muscles in check and not burst out laughing.

I grabbed my book bag and headed up to my room. Dad was right behind me.

"You'll have a good time tonight," he said. "Even if Aunt Maude's digestive problems are causing her to bubble and squeak."

"Very funny," I said. "You're going to owe me for this. Like a fantastic sweet sixteen birthday. In three weeks."

"Hey," Dad said, "I've got it. What does Savvy sound like when she's been overchewing her gum? Bubble and squeak."

"Not funny, Dad." I tossed my books in the corner as Mom came in for a quick vote of approval on her outfit.

"Looks great, Mom," I said. "Can I come?"

She grinned. "Nope!"

They kissed Louanne good-bye and headed downstairs and into London for the night.

"So what shall we do?" Aunt Maude said once Louanne and I returned to the kitchen. Aunt Maude had already cut up half a chicken breast for Growl, his favorite, and he was resting contentedly on the back of the couch. "The bubble and squeak is boiling away. I've got some lovely ideas for afters, but we have some time to kill first." She peered out the window into the back garden area. "Well, hardly a thing has been done since we cleaned it up last month. Mum pretty busy?"

I made eye contact with Louanne, who looked back at me. I wasn't exactly sure how much to tell her.

Chapter 46

"Well, there've been a lot of expenses this spring," I began.

"I see." Aunt Maude appeared to be thinking hard. Then she turned the heat down on the bubble and squeak and said to us, "You know, the British government requires that landlords invest a certain amount of money into their properties each year. Now I try not to grumble, as you know, but with the many ailments I must bear, it's been difficult for me to decide what to do here. I've got just the idea. Let's buy some roses and put them back there for your mum."

"Actually, Mom has a notebook of plants she'd like," Louanne said. "It's in the drawer by the microwave if you want to see it."

I closed my eyes and cringed. You didn't tell someone what to buy as a present! When I opened my eyes again, though, Aunt Maude didn't seem to be put out at all. Which was sweet!

"Certainly she would have ideas about what she'd fancy. Well, come along then; let's go. I've got to come back and make a mess very soon, so there's no time to waste."

"A mess?" I inquired. Normally Aunt Maude bustled about cleaning up, not making a mess.

She grabbed her keys and threw me an I'm-so-sorry-you're-an-undercultured-American look. "Yes, dear, Eton mess. Strawberries, meringue, and cream."

After the dinner of bubble and squeak—aka cabbage and potatoes—followed by the mess, Aunt Maude informed us that she was going to make a dessert for my parents to eat when they arrived tomorrow, and would I please look through her cookery book to find something? "You do cook, don't you?" she asked.

"Nope," I said.

"She'd better learn," Louanne teased. "She's got her first boyfriend now."

"Ou'reyay eadday," I said under my breath.

"My, my," Aunt Maude said. "And of course it's a British boy. Vastly superior to all others in every way," she said, clucking. "I'm sure he's quite handsome."

"She's got a snap of him on her phone," Louanne volunteered before she ditched from the room.

"Well, then, let's have a look," Aunt Maude said.

I pulled out my phone and scrolled through till I got a good close-up of Tommy, and then I handed the phone to her.

She stared at him for quite a while, her face going from teasingly positive to almost shocked. For a minute I wondered if her digestive system was kicking up again. "He's very handsome," she said. "It's Tommy, right?"

Now it was my turn to be shocked. "Yes. Do you know him?"

"Never met him," she said. And as much as I pressed, and later even sent Louanne to press, she would say no more.

Chapter 47

Friday, no-uniform day. To distract myself from my biggest worry—how to angle the article to completely engage a bunch of my classmates with summer fever—I spent an extra hour planning what to wear.

I had a white hoodie that I loved—Hollister Malibu with red and black lettering—and I hadn't worn my black and gray checked Vans for a while. But what jeans? Sighing, I took out my second-best pair and slipped them on. Not for the first time since the Great Laundry Disaster, I mourned the loss of my best jeans.

On the way to school, I started thinking about the article again. I just saw no way out of it, and I started getting mad. Why should my entire career ride on one article at the end of the year? Ridiculous.

Just before I got to Wexburg Academy, I received a text. It was from Supriya.

Don't worry about anything; instead, pray about everything. Tell God what you need, and thank him for all he has done. Philippians 4:6

Lord, thank You for helping me with everything so far. I really want to write this article—and to have a permanent spot on the newspaper staff next year, which I'd really love. Thanks again.

Just before I walked into the building, I added, *And I'd like Tommy to ask me to go out with him. If that's not too much to ask.*

The first three periods went by quickly. I'd been planning to sit at the newspaper table that day to pick Melissa's brain about angle ideas— after all, I had only three or four days to get the whole thing written—but she wasn't there. Hazelle told me that both Melissa and Jack were at some meeting for sixth formers. And then—a surprise.

"Can I talk with you in the courtyard?" Hazelle asked.

I nodded and we stepped outside together.

"Savvy . . . well, maybe you were right," she began. "The Asking for Trouble column is very important to the paper. And if I want to do what's right for the paper, I guess we'd better keep it. So if you still want to write it, you can."

I felt dizzy. I was keeping the column! "I'd like to keep it. Thank you, Hazelle."

Hazelle looked wrung out. I suspected she was facing a few testing moments of her own. "And about the other article—the one Jack promised you. You're right about journalistic integrity. So you can do one article."

"On what topic?" I asked, hardly daring to hope.

"Whatever you want," Hazelle said. "If the article is a success—if it creates buzz, causes an effect, brings in letters to the editor—I'll let you write regularly next school term. You can have articles under your own name and with your own byline. And if it isn't a success, then I won't. But you'll still have the advice column. Agreed?"

She'd said it was all about the paper, nothing personal, and she was keeping it that way. "Deal," I said, wondering how an article about a ministry was going to generate buzz that would be heard at the end of the school term, when all anyone wanted to do was finish up their work and get on with holidays.

But fair was fair. The challenge was on.

I headed back into the lunchroom and slid in alongside Penny, which was always fun, except that she was sitting in the middle that day. Which meant we were right across from Ashley, who was holding court and complaining about something while everyone mewed sympathetically. This time, though, I could relate.

"I still haven't found any jeans I like," she said. "If they fit in the waist, they don't fit in the leg or hip. I can't for the life of me understand why it's so difficult to get a pair that works all at once. And I don't want to wear something that everyone else is wearing either."

I looked around the table, and everyone was nodding, tossing out brand names and their general dissatisfaction. I completely agreed.

And then I had an idea. I just didn't know how to bring it together. I tuned everyone out and tried to figure out the details, but I couldn't.

Two are better than one.

I leaned toward Penny. "Are you busy after school?"

"I've got a few minutes, but then I've got to go to the dentist," she said. "Why?"

"Okay. Let's talk after sixth period." We both had Miss Nodding.

Penny agreed, and I counted the hours.

Chapter 48

After a history class full of cheerful recounting of the Great Plague of London in 1665, complete with running sores, bleeding from the ears, and putrid stenches, I was ready to present my fabulous idea to Penny. We grabbed our book bags and headed out of class.

"You know how Ashley was saying at lunch that she had no jeans and how both Alison and I had to put our jeans back when we were in London because Ashley couldn't find anything?"

"Are you still not over that?" Penny teased.

"Kind of," I admitted. "Anyway, I think most of us have a hard time finding great jeans. And who wants to pay a hundred pounds for a pair of jeans that doesn't fit perfectly? But I also don't want to wear jeans that make me look like Farmer Brown."

"Agreed." Penny wasn't pushing me, though I could tell by the blank look on her face that she wasn't tracking yet.

"So . . . when I was working with Becky, she sent me home with a stack of catalogs. I looked through them and found a lot of cool things, of course. One of the coolest was for a company that licenses out the right to make custom-fit jeans. The retailer—in this case, Be@titude—buys a license to sell custom jeans within a certain area, like Wexburg plus twenty kilometers all around. Then they get the exclusive right to custom-fit jeans for anyone. A perfect fit. So what if I asked Becky if she'd be willing to be the licensee for this area, and we put that in my article, and then a lot of people went into her store to buy the jeans?"

A little smile appeared on Penny's face, but she wasn't exactly jumping up and down with enthusiasm like I'd hoped she would be. "What makes you think people will run right out and buy them, even if it's in the article?"

"We'll take a picture of someone wearing the jeans. Like . . . you!" I said. "You could wear them, and we'll take a snap of it and run it alongside the article with some comments from you."

Penny giggled. "Thanks, Savvy, but I doubt if hordes of people are going to descend upon the shop just because I'm wearing the jeans. Now, if it were someone like Ashley . . ."

We sat on a bench at the edge of campus. "You want me to give Ashley *more* publicity?"

"I want you to give the *shop* more publicity," Penny said.

I nodded. "Yes . . . that does make sense. And if Ashley likes them, everyone else will too."

"Exactly," Penny said. "But you have two hurdles before you can even get to that point. Getting Ashley to agree to model them. And getting Becky to take the risk on investing in the license."

Chapter 49

I decided to text Ashley.

> Hey, Ashley, it's Savvy. I wondered if you had a minute to meet me so I could talk about an idea with you. It's about fashion, so of course I thought of you.

Hey, I wasn't above a little ego stroking for a good cause.

She texted me back a few minutes later.

> All right. You can come by tomorrow morning after ten. I'll alert the butler to expect you.

Hooray! I had an audience with the queen.

My chauffeur—um, Dad—drove me to The Beeches after breakfast. Well, after *their* breakfast. I was too excited and worried to eat. I'd brought the catalog to show Ashley . . . even though I hadn't asked Becky yet. To be honest, I wasn't sure whom I should ask first. If Ashley wasn't behind it, then I couldn't ask Becky to waste her licensing money. But if Ashley said yes and then Becky said no, Ashley was going to be peeved, to put it politely.

"I'll just park down here then, miss, shall I?" Dad said.

"Ha-ha," I said. "Quit joking and start praying!"

I hopped out of the car and walked up the long two flights of buttery stone steps toward the double-door entrance to The Beeches. I didn't even need to tap on the door knocker. As soon as I reached the top flight, the butler opened the door.

"Hullo, miss. Miss Ashley is expecting you in the sitting room." He indicated the pinkish room to his right. I'd been there before, months ago, when The Beeches had been having an open house for the National Trust.

I headed in that direction, wishing like everything that my shoes didn't squeak like sick ducks every time I stepped on the polished wood floor. The door was already open, and Ashley was sitting at a large mahogany desk with a brand-new computer, doing her homework.

"Hullo, Savvy," she said, her voice neither warm nor cold. "Come on over here." She indicated an upholstered wing chair near her seat.

"Thanks," I said. "I have an idea—a fashion idea—that I'd like to share with you." I ran down the details as I'd explained them to Penny, leaving out the fact that I'd asked Penny to model first. "Because you're very fashion forward, I thought of you to model them. Last time we featured The Beeches in the newspaper, there was a great response. I have every reason to believe we'd have the same response this time."

Ashley nodded at me. "I can see why you'd like to have me model," she said. "So you're suggesting The Beeches for the launch, then?"

Launch? I hadn't even thought of a launch, but I wasn't going to let her know that. Nor would I ever have had the nerve to suggest The Beeches for anything. But if she was suggesting it . . . I worked really hard at keeping my forty-three muscles straight. "If you think it's a good idea, then of course I agree," I said.

"It'd have to be next Saturday in order to get it done before the end of the year," she said. "A week from today. And your article is coming out . . . ?"

"This Thursday. Two days before the launch." *Please, God, let Becky say yes, or else I'm dead and you might as well just get a broom and sweep me up. Ashes to ashes and all that.* "Is that too short notice for your mom to get things ready?"

Ashley laughed. "My mum doesn't get things ready, Savvy. We have staff."

I almost mentioned that Be@titude was the store that lost all of its computer stuff because of her e-card, but I didn't think that guilting someone into anything was good form. Not that it would be successful with Ashley anyway. I'd learned my lesson, and I let God work.

A minute went by, then two. I could hear "the staff" putting away the breakfast service in the dining room nearby.

"All right," she said. "I'll do it. I'll talk with my mum about the launch and text you shortly."

"That is *so* great!" I said. "Thank you so much.

I mean, it's going to be like you're wearing a Stella McCartney."

"No need to pour it on, Savvy. I've already agreed," she said, but not too unkindly.

I had to stop myself from hugging the butler on the way out the door.

Chapter 50

"Please take me directly to Be@titude, Jensen," I said, playing along with Dad as chauffeur.

He pulled his hat down over his eyes. "Right away, ma'am," he said.

As he drove, I prayed. And it didn't take long to get to the shop. We pulled up outside in less than five minutes.

I pushed open the door and saw that Becky was helping a customer check out. She looked up at me and smiled, her face not showing any anger or resentment over the computer issue. When her customer left, she greeted me warmly. "Hey, Savvy!"

I nearly collapsed in tears to hear her welcome.

"Becky, do you have a few minutes?" I asked, pulling myself together.

"Sure," she said.

I set her stack of catalogs on the counter, with the custom jeans one on top. "I have an idea," I started, "though I don't know what you'll think." I reminded myself to speak slowly, and then I ran over everything I'd talked about with Penny and with Ashley. "Ashley said she'd check to see if the launch could be at The Beeches. It would give us the best chance. Do you know the Gorm Strausses?"

Becky smiled. "We all know the Gorm Strausses. So I'd have to pay the licensing fee of . . . ?"

"Three hundred pounds," I said. "I know. It's a lot. And there's not much time to get everything together because you'd have to contact them and see if the license is available, and then if they could bring samples up for the launch. But you did say you wanted teens to come into the shop more. Right? This is the way to do it."

Becky sat there for a minute, considering. Then she said, "Let's pray."

I closed my eyes, and she prayed, asking the Lord if this was the direction He was leading and, if so, to let us know. I opened my eyes, and she said, "There are still some things I need to check out . . . but I think it's a go."

"Hooray!" I shouted, and at that moment I got a text from Ashley.

> Mum says fine. We'll take care of details on this end. Can do photo shoot on Tuesday if you can get the jeans to me by then.

I handed my phone over to Becky so she could read it.

She nodded firmly. "I'll work on getting the jeans here."

"I'll work on the article," I said, passionately hoping that a lot of people would read it and show up—for Becky, of course, but also for my future with the Wexburg Academy *Times*.

"What should we call it?" Becky asked. "Perfect Fit?"

"That's a bit old for teenagers. How about . . ." I racked my brain. And then it came to me. The perfect name for a line of custom-fit jeans.

"How about InJeanious?"

Chapter 51

At church on Sunday I shared the news with Supriya and the worship team. They all promised to pray about my article and for the success of the event. After Sunday school, Tommy came up to me, and I told him the details I hadn't been able to via text.

"So," he said, "are guys invited to this?"

"Absolutely. They wear jeans, don't they?"

He nodded. "And would one need a date for this event?"

I grinned. It wouldn't be one-on-one, after all. "I don't know if one would, but some might."

"Do you need a date?" he teased.

"Yes . . . if the right person asks."

Monday at school, Tommy showed up carrying a sticky paper with the words *Right Person* on it. He stuck it on his shirt and said, "Would you like to go to the launch with me on Saturday?"

I took the sticky paper off his shirt. "Absolutely!"

I was psyched, of course. But he still hadn't officially asked me out.

Chapter 52

Tuesday afternoon I turned in my copy to Hazelle. "Let's read it together in my office," she said. Her voice was professional but not unfriendly, and I had the feeling that we'd both been through a lot. Maybe we could someday find our way back to friendship.

She rolled her eyes when she read my lead-in.

"'Due to unforeseen circumstances, this paper is unable to have a horoscope column this week. In its place, we'd like to present a *hero*scope— someone who is working hard to make Wexburg a better place for all of us.'

"Oh, Savvy," she said, but she didn't use her red pencil to mark it out. She did make a few little tweaks throughout, making sure it was clear that the entire school was invited to the launch on Saturday, whether or not they planned to buy jeans.

"Will they be able to order jeans at the launch? Will there be a place to be measured?"

I nodded. "Ashley's getting that all set up, and Becky's going to be there, along with some of her designer friends, to measure a few people."

"Let's word it this way, then," Hazelle said, drawing a few lines to rearrange a paragraph.

She didn't touch the part promising fun under twinkling lights and butler service. "I guess I should be there," she said, trying, I knew, to look reluctant. "As the editor, and all."

"Of course," I said. "I'll have Ashley's snaps to you first thing in the morning. Here's the one of the little girl I mentioned in the article." I pushed Emma's photo toward her.

♡

Thursday morning I got in even earlier than usual. I wasn't going to wait to deliver the paper to read this article. And I wanted to set aside fifteen of the best copies for myself and my family, just in case I never wrote another article with a byline.

Tears sprang when I saw the copy. Hazelle had put it on the front page.

Like Your @titude! by Savvy Smith

Need new jeans but haven't got time to head into London? Want to make a difference right where you live? Like parties but have nothing going on this weekend?

Now you can solve all three of those problems with one fabbo night out at The Beeches. Come and enjoy a night of music, dancing, fun, and fashion as local shop Be@titude helps both guys and girls slip into custom-fit jeans from its new InJeanious line.

"To be quite honest, I've never really liked denim," says socialite Ashley Gorm Strauss. "Many jeans have a common cut. However, the new line by InJeanious helps each person design something uniquely theirs. Everyone will be wearing a pair by next school year. I guarantee it."

A portion of each sale of jeans goes toward a professional wardrobe for local single mums—so you can feel good while you're looking good. Here are some of the things you can expect:

Chapter 53

It was Friday night, and everything was set. The samples were all at Be@titude, ready to be shuttled over to The Beeches the next day. Ashley's staff had turned several of the rooms on the lower floor into swanky try-on rooms, and she'd told me that their cook had prepared lots of snacks for a huge help-yourself buffet table.

I had my outfit—a sample pair of the InJeanious jeans that I was hoping to buy. If I could score a summer job. I had my date—though we were meeting there, and I knew I'd be busy with details. I had my bestie. I was set.

I sat in my room that night praying all would go well. And then I broke out my guitar to soothe myself. I thumbed through some music and finally settled on Taylor Swift's "Fifteen." Because fifteen was slipping away from me. I had high hopes for the night—and the year ahead.

Chapter 54

When Ashley had set the party time for later in the evening, I hadn't really understood why she'd wanted to do that. Would people be kind of tired? Did the Gorm Strausses want to save on food expenses? That hardly seemed likely. But when Mom and I pulled up to The Beeches, I knew right away why she'd set it for later.

The driveway was lit on each side from end to end—it must have been half a mile or more through the amazing beech trees, which stood like more of their staff lining the drive. When the house came into view, it, too, was ablaze from every window. But most beautiful of all were the trees—in the front garden and on the back property—which twinkled with rice lights, like millions of fireflies had settled contentedly on each branch.

"Wow," I said, in spite of my desire to remain cool.

"Wow," Mom said. I had to admit, she looked pretty spiffy herself. Penny's mum had called her to tell her that the parents were welcome in the west wing of the estate to have some appetizers and to talk. Penny told me the real reasons why they were invited, though:

1. We couldn't drive ourselves yet.
2. We needed their cheque books.

We'd arrived earlier than most so I could help Becky with last-minute prep. Mom headed off with the other parents, and as she did, I heard Penny's mum talking excitedly about the garden club and the tours they were planning for the summer. Judging by the positive chatter, she had no concerns at all that my mom would be voted in. I felt happy for my mother.

"Hullo, Savvy," Ashley said. Well, Becky had done exactly what we'd decided ahead of time, although I had to admit to a slight twinge of envy. She'd given Ashley the very best jean style and had also thrown in a top and a set of flats from one of her designer friends.

"You look stunning," I said. And I meant it. It was good for business. Everyone would want to be dressed like Ashley.

"The outfit is rather smart, isn't it?" she agreed. "I've got to get back to the dining room, where we've set up an order table for those wanting to place orders tonight. Becky is just around there, putting things up in the sitting room, the music room, and the library."

Within the hour Penny arrived, and she and I helped Becky and her friends finish the setup. In no time at all, the house and the grounds were packed with people. Guys, girls, parents with cash—everyone imaginable.

I had just helped one girl sort through some styles for a personalized try-on when I felt a hand on my shoulder.

"Hey, there."

I turned around. It was Tommy. "Hey," I said, unable to stop the happiness from spreading up to my face and blossoming into a big smile. "I was wondering when you'd get here."

He rolled his eyes. "My grandparents were going to drive me, and then my dad got home in time, but my gran didn't want to miss the chance to eat free at The Beeches, so now the whole clan is here. Thankfully my sister had a date or they'd have packed her along too." He glanced around the room. "By the look of things, it's going brilliantly!"

I grinned. "It seems that way, but I'm not willing to declare victory till we count the orders at the end of the night—and till I hear the word *victory* from Hazelle's lips."

"Is she here yet?"

I shook my head. "I don't think so. I haven't seen her, but in a crowd this big . . ." I shrugged.

"Savvy!" Becky called out to me. "I could use a hand if you've got a spare one."

"I'll meet you outside after things die down," Tommy said. "Text me when you've got a minute. I, uh, want to talk."

"Okay," I said, jumpy as those firefly lights. I hoped I knew what he was going to say.

He started toward the buffet, where his football friends were. Then he turned back to me once more. At first I was embarrassed that I was still looking at him. And then he winked.

He winked! *My* wink! The long-awaited wink.

I practically floated to Becky and helped her

organize the orders she was taking. Just as I finished alphabetizing them, I felt a tap and spun around. It was Hazelle, and she had a serious expression on her face. "Savvy. I need to talk with you. Is there somewhere kind of private?"

Chapter 55

What could Hazelle have to tell me in private other than something bad—and bad about the newspaper? She was probably going to tell me that Natalie was back on the staff, and because she had seniority, she was going to have to take the staff writer position. Or maybe someone else found out that I was the Asking for Trouble columnist and it was going to be all over campus next week. Or something worse! The rumor would run through the crowd at the launch and steal the thunder from InJeanious.

"Savvy!" Hazelle said sharply. "Is there somewhere we can go to talk?"

I popped out of my bubble. "Oh, sure, right. Here's the storage area for the sample jeans. It's pretty private." We walked to the closet, and I closed the door behind us. "What's up?" I braced myself for her answer.

"Brian's here," she said.

"Okay . . ." I was waiting for the rest.

"He's here. And so is everyone else, but he's here. And, well, you always wanted to make me over. Now's your chance."

I exercised extreme control over my forty-three facial muscles. "Sure . . . I mean, if that's what you want."

"I do," she said. I'd already taken care of everything Becky had asked me to do, so we sorted through the stack of jeans till we found something that was pretty close to an ideal fit. And then I ran and got one of the designer shirts that Ashley had rejected before settling on her perfect look. I hustled back to the closet, threw it at Hazelle, and closed the door on her. A few minutes later she came out. "Well?"

"Fabulous," I pronounced. "Let me tweak your makeup just a little bit and twist your hair to the side." What I really wanted was a straightening iron, but there wasn't one here. "Okay, kid, go get 'em," I said.

I stood back and watched as she approached

232

the buffet room. Heads turned and conversation quieted as she walked by. I felt just like a mother hen. I had my moment, then went back to help Becky and the designers. Ashley did her bit by floating through the rooms and the gardens, looking amazing.

And then there was Hazelle. Her makeover was intended to stun Brian, but it had a much bigger effect. I even heard a few people say, "If those jeans can make Hazelle look that good, sign me up!"

A few hours later, the music died down some, and about half the people melted away. Becky came up and pulled me aside. "Savvy, guess what?"

"What?"

"Look at this number."

Chapter 56

I couldn't believe the bottom line. "No way. Is that the whole order?"

She shook her head. "It's not even the total. There are still people in line. And that's only orders from tonight. We've got a six-month license, so when they love the jeans and want another pair, they'll have to come back to Be@titude."

"Is that enough money for the clothing program for single mothers?"

"More than enough," Becky said as she squeezed my arm. "But I'll be really busy. I might need some help at the shop this summer. Know anyone who'd like a job in fashion?"

I grinned. "I'm sure I can come up with someone."

"You might not need the money," she said, "after your cut."

My mouth dropped open. "My cut?"

"Sure," she said. "You'll get a small commission on the orders. I'd guess about—" she did a couple of calculations and wrote a number on a piece of paper—"this much."

"Really?"

"Really. Just don't blow it all on clothes," she teased.

I laughed. A picture of Emma crawling under the rounders at the shop passed through my mind.

"Some of it on clothes. And some on a play-house."

Now it was her turn to be shocked. "A play-house?"

"I'll tell you later." I waved and headed out of the room to text Tommy.

I have some time—where should I meet you?

Back garden, left corner. By the roses.

I glanced in the mirror. A little disheveled, but it would have to do for now. On the way out the door, I saw Hazelle and gave her a thumbs-up. I'd hoped to walk by, but she came up to talk with me. I didn't want my anxiety to show, but apparently it did.

"Are you okay?" she asked. "You looked nervous when I saw you before, and you look nervous now."

"Well, to be honest, when I saw you the first time, I was a little worried you were going to tell me bad news about the paper," I admitted.

"Bad news?" she asked. "There were hundreds of people here. Plus, I've already received like eight letters to the editor, and that was before the event. You have nothing to worry about."

"Really?"

"Really," she said. "And after tonight . . . well, I'm wondering if maybe we might need to run a regular feature on fashion."

"Great idea," I said. "I have some suggestions. . . ."

She held up her hand. "I just said I was wondering, Savvy, not committing. Don't run ahead of me."

I laughed. It was good to know that, great jeans or not, Hazelle was still Hazelle. "What did Brian think?"

"He said I looked great and tried to start a conversation with me twice. But you know, I told him it's over." She looked happy and confident. I leaned over and hugged her.

Talking about Brian reminded me . . . I had an appointment. "I gotta run," I said. "Talk to you later."

I made my way through the thinning crowd toward the back of the garden, where the prize-winning Gorm Strauss rose garden was aglow with the twinkling lights. I saw Tommy sitting on a bench, and I came over and sat next to him. Close, but not too close.

He smiled when he saw me. "Big success, eh?"

I nodded. "I am so happy for Becky. I am so thankful to God."

"So, Savvy—" he took my hand in his, and I didn't pull it away—"I was wondering. Do your parents mind if you go out with people?"

"No." I was glad I'd already talked it over with Mom.

The music drifted out from the house, and there were some crickets trying their best to keep time in the distance. "Would you go out with me, then?" he asked.

"Yes, I will."

He leaned just a little bit toward me.

I instantly recognized the pose, of course. Dude decoder!

"Do you mind if I kiss you?" he asked.

"No," I said. I closed my eyes, and he leaned over and lightly brushed his lips against mine. That was it. I didn't expect it to happen often, and I knew that till my wedding day, there'd be nothing more. But I was not going to be "sweet sixteen and never been kissed."

As I opened my eyes, I saw him bending over. He plucked a rose from one of the bushes and handed it to me. "Don't tell Ashley's mum," he said.

I laughed. As I did, I heard a man behind me clearing his throat.

Chapter 57

I turned around. "Father Christmas!" How long had he been there, and what had he seen?

"Grandpa!" Tommy said.

I turned and looked at Tommy. "Grandpa?"

"Yeah, that's my grandpa," he said. "You know each other?"

"Uh, kind of," I said. "I interviewed him for the paper." I hoped I hadn't spilled his secret.

Father Christmas seemed to know what I was thinking. "Don't worry; he knows about me," he said. "A bit hard to keep that kind of secret from your own family."

Well, that would explain how Tommy's gran knew about my writing for the paper. Father Christmas—also known as Tom, the postmaster—was the one who had brought a pen to me on Christmas Day. "Oh . . . I see." I was finally connecting the dots. "Your name is Tom," I said to him. "Aunt Maude called you Tom."

His eyes twinkled, just like Father Christmas's should. "Aunt Maude, eh? We called her Mad Maude in my day. She was quite the social butterfly."

"Social butterfly?"

He smiled. "I dated her a bit meself before she ran off and got married to a man from up north. Then I met Tommy's gran, and the rest is history." Another mystery solved. Aunt Maude recognized Tommy because, well, he did look like his grandfather. Much cuter, though. Of course.

"So how are you doing on those Christmas wishes?" he asked.

"What were those?" Tommy asked me.

Oh no. I was going to have to be brutally honest because Father Christmas would surely remember everything I'd said. I took a deep breath. "I asked for a really good friend; a guy who likes me for myself; a place, or two, to do good work; and . . . a Wexburg Academy *Times* pen."

"And how are you doing on lining those up?" Father Christmas asked.

I grinned but refused to look at Tommy. "I, uh . . . They all seem to be lining up pretty well now."

"You're a quick study," Father Christmas—I mean, Postmaster Tom, or, uh, Tommy's grandfather, said. "You'll have to set some new goals. You can tell me all about them. In December." He turned to Tommy. "I came to find you, as it's time to go. Are you and your young lady ready?"

His young lady! I held the rose stem loosely in my hand. "I'm ready."

Then we three walked back to The Beeches together, under the stars—both electric and natural—chatting and laughing like you should when you live in jolly old England.

Later that night, when I was home and nearly asleep, I thought of the perfect way to end the night. I dug out my phone and typed in a verse. Then I forwarded it to everyone I knew.

"For I know the plans I have for you," says the Lord. "They are plans for good and not for disaster, to give you a future and a hope." Jeremiah 29:11

Your Father, who sees what is done in secret, will reward you.

MATTHEW 6:4 (NIV)